HOPES AND DREAMS

What Reviewers Say About PJ Trebelhorn's Work

On the Fly

"This was such an easy book to love. The story flowed beautifully, characters were really well developed, and I couldn't put it down from the minute I started it. I also think it was really excellent how engaged I was in the sections that concentrated on ice hockey even though it is not a sport I know well."—*Les Rêveur*

Twice in a Lifetime

"*Twice in a Lifetime* is a sweet and easy read with two likable characters whom readers will root for. Featuring a widow and a police officer who share the same tragedy, the book deals with their intertwining backstory tenderly and thoughtfully. *Twice in a Lifetime* also features a compelling antagonist, a welcome dash of action and great explorations of power dynamics within lesbian relationships."—*RT Book Reviews*

The Right Kind of Wrong

"[A] nice, gentle read with some great secondary characters, easy pacing, and a pleasant writing style. Something you could happily read on a lazy Sunday afternoon."—*Rainbow Book Reviews*

"PJ Trebelhorn has written a romantic, sexy story with just the right amount of angst."—*Kitty Kat's Book Review Blog*

"Quinn has had her heart broken in the past and to avoid it happening again decides to enjoy life as a player. She's always had feelings for her best friend Grace but when they met they decided to be friends and Quinn will always honor that commitment. Grace however is only now realizing twenty years later that she has maybe had feelings for Quinn all along...but can she take a chance on them losing their very close friendship? The love story between these two characters is well formed and you can understand their feelings for one another as well as knowing the inner turmoil of potentially losing your best friend..." —*Les Rêveur*

Taking a Gamble

"This is a truly superb feel-good novel. Ms Trebelhorn is obviously an accomplished writer of engaging and riveting tales. Not only is this a very readable novel but it is full of humour and convincing, beautifully written and conceived realities about falling in love for the first time."—*Inked Rainbow Reads*

Desperate Measures

"I love kick-ass police detectives especially when they're women. This book contains a superior specimen of the breed."—*Rainbow Book Reviews*

From This Moment On

"*From This Moment On* is a fine read for coping with loss as well as being a touching lesbian romance tale."—*Midwest Book Review*

"...Trebelhorn created characters for *From This Moment On* that are flawed, faulted and wholly realistic: While many of the characters are struggling with loss, their unique approaches to dealing with it reveal their weaknesses and give the reader a deeper appreciation of the characters...*From This Moment On*... tells a gripping, emotional story about love, loss and the fusion of the two."—*Philadelphia Gay News*

By the Author

HOPES AND DREAMS

by

PJ Trebelhorn

2020

HOPES AND DREAMS

ISBN 13: 978-1-63555-670-4

This Trade Paperback Original Is Published By
Bold Strokes Books, Inc.
P.O. Box 249
Valley Falls, NY 12185

First Edition: August 2020

CREDITS
EDITOR: CINDY CRESAP
PRODUCTION DESIGN: SUSAN RAMUNDO
COVER DESIGN BY TAMMY SEIDICK

Acknowledgments

My eternal thanks to Radclyffe, Sandy Lowe, and everyone at Bold Strokes Books who make this such an incredible family to be a part of. You're all amazing!

To my editor, Cindy Cresap, thank you doesn't seem to be enough for all you do. The notes you send with my edits always make me smile.

To my wife, Cheryl, I can't put into words how much your support means to me. You are my rock, and I'm incredibly blessed to have you in my life.

A special thank you to all the women and men on the front lines fighting the battle that is Covid-19. You are all appreciated and loved.

And last but not least, a huge thank you to you, the readers. You all keep me on my toes and every note of encouragement serves to remind me why I love to write.

Dedication

For Cheryl, Always

PROLOGUE

R iley Warren stared, transfixed by the aftermath of the horrific crash she'd just witnessed. The brand-new Mercedes she'd been admiring from directly behind it was broadsided as it pulled away from the stop sign. The pickup that hit it hadn't had its headlights on, and it never even slowed down for its stop sign. The Mercedes was off the road after being pushed quite a few feet, and the driver of the pickup had been thrown through his windshield, obviously having not been wearing his seat belt. He wasn't moving from where he landed about twenty feet from the Mercedes, and Riley guessed he was probably dead.

She could hear absolutely nothing but the pounding of her own heart, but she realized she wasn't breathing and forced herself to start. She fumbled for the phone in her pocket but never took her eyes off the scene. It was dark and there were no other cars on the road. Not surprising since Riley was on her way home from work and it was almost one o'clock in the morning. She quickly gave the information to the 911 operator but dropped her phone when she saw what looked like the beginning of a fire inside the Mercedes.

Without giving much thought to what she was doing, she jumped out of her car and ran toward the accident. There was no way an ambulance was going to make it here in time to rescue the driver if those were indeed flames she was seeing. She was pretty sure cars didn't really explode after an accident like they did in the movies, but just in case, she knew she needed to get the driver out.

The window was shattered, but there was no way she was going to get the door open since that was where the pickup had hit it, so she pulled out the pocketknife she always carried with her and quickly sliced through the seat belt.

"Can you hear me?" she asked, ignoring the heat coming from the flames which hadn't yet overtaken everything. Maybe she could get this person out before it got too bad if she was lucky. It was a woman and she was groaning, but she didn't seem to be fully aware of her surroundings. Riley took a deep breath and maneuvered herself so she could get her arms under the woman's and tried to pull her out. She wasn't budging. "Ma'am, you have to wake up. You need to get out of the car now!"

"What?" the woman said, looking around in a daze before apparently realizing she was in grave danger. She looked up at Riley, but Riley couldn't see her face very well because it was covered in blood from a cut somewhere on her head.

"Can you move?" Riley asked, wondering how in the world she was able to remain so calm in the midst of the chaos surrounding her. She took a moment to wipe the blood from the woman's eyes. They looked familiar somehow, but she didn't know of anyone in town who had enough money to afford a Mercedes, new or not. Well, except for the Thayers, but she didn't want to think about that as a possibility. She shook her head. None of it mattered. She needed to get this woman out now.

"Yes," she said and nodded her head. Her eyes were wild and full of fear, and before Riley could even try to pull her once more, she started screaming and kicking her legs. The fire had finally reached her.

Riley tugged again, and probably because the woman was now kicking her legs, was able to pull her out. She used her jacket to put out the flames on her legs before dragging her about twenty feet away in case the whole thing did actually go up. She finally let her go and fell back onto her ass, completely out of breath.

The woman was passed out now, but whether it was from pain or exhaustion Riley couldn't say. She maneuvered herself so she sat with the woman's head in her lap, not wanting to leave her in case she woke up again. Riley knew *she* wouldn't want to be alone had their roles been reversed. She spared a glance at the man who had been driving the pickup, but she was now sure he was dead. No doubt drunk, too. He hadn't moved, and his body was at an unnatural angle. She looked down at the woman again and wiped away more of the blood from her face.

Riley's heart lurched, and her breath caught as she finally recognized the face. It *was* one of the Thayers. But was it Victoria or Vanessa? They were identical twins, and Riley hadn't seen either of them in nearly twenty years. Not since their high school graduation. If it was Vanessa, and had she known beforehand, she might have thought twice about reaching into a burning car to save her. She looked at her own arm and saw it was pretty badly burned. Probably from when she was putting the fire out on the woman since the flames hadn't reached where her arms were before she got her out of the car.

She glanced over her shoulder when she heard sirens approaching but still didn't move until one of the paramedics, Megan Wilson, her best friend, came running over to where she was sitting in the middle of the road.

"Jesus Christ, what the hell happened here?" she asked, dropping to her knees and seeing the condition of whichever Thayer sister was in Riley's arms. She met Riley's eyes. "You're burned too. Are you all right?"

"I'm fine," Riley answered, waving her off. She knew when her adrenaline high wore off she'd be in a world of hurt, but until then she was okay playing the hero. "She needs a lot of help though."

"Don't move," Megan said with a quick nod before she ran over to check on the other driver. Riley saw her shake her head, then Megan ran back to her rig to get what she needed to help, stopping briefly to give directions to her partner. Riley had never been more grateful her best friend and roommate was an EMT. Unless this was Vanessa. Riley chuckled and shook her head because she knew it wouldn't have mattered. It wasn't in her nature to not help someone in need.

But damn, it was just nice to fantasize for a moment.

Chapter One

One Year Later

Victoria Thayer looked at the time on the laptop she was using to answer her email. She was not looking forward to going back to the house she'd grown up in, a place she hadn't visited since graduating college sixteen years ago. Her mother, Vera, had made it perfectly clear she wasn't welcome there after coming out to her and her father. And now, at Vanessa's request, she was going there for a three-week stay leading up to Vanessa's wedding.

Vanessa had been her best friend as well as her identical twin sister while they were growing up, and she'd never been able to deny her anything. Even if it meant dealing with Vera again for an entire three weeks it seemed. She'd taken to calling her mother Vera when she'd made it clear she no longer saw Vic as her daughter.

Her father, on the other hand, had been nothing but supportive of Vic, always. She loved him, and she'd loved his parents as well. Her grandfather had started the Thayer Group when he'd been twenty-two years old, and he'd grown it into a multi-billion-dollar company by the time he'd passed away. They'd started with luxury hotels, but spread out to restaurants and, more recently, day spas. As a result, they now had more money than they knew what to do with.

Vic had always loved when they'd visited her grandparents. Their house was always so full of positive feelings, unlike the house she'd grown up in. She closed her laptop and stood to look out at the view of New York City through the floor to ceiling windows in her office. She sighed heavily and rested her forehead against the glass. She was so tired of this life. She knew a lot of people would give anything to have her position and wealth, but she'd never truly been happy working as the head of marketing for the Thayer Group. Her passion was in her painting, even if she never sold another piece. She often thought she'd be perfectly happy living somewhere secluded spending her days doing nothing but painting.

"Daydreaming again?" Vanessa asked as she walked into the office without knocking. Vic turned to face her and gave her a weary smile. Vanessa walked over to her and placed a hand on her arm. "Or are you just dreading going back to Wolf Bay?"

"Not Wolf Bay, per se," she said with a shrug. "But home. To *Vera's* home. I don't know how you managed to talk me into spending three weeks there."

"I want you there with me, you know that." Vanessa moved to sit on the couch along the far wall and crossed her legs.

Vic smiled and wondered at the fact they were identical twins, but so different in how they presented themselves. Vanessa got most of the feminine traits, and Vic was definitely more on the butch side. Vanessa's blond hair was long and stylish, and Vic's was short and stylishly messy. Before her accident, Vanessa had worn dresses and skirts as often as she could, and Vic hadn't worn one since her high school graduation. She was much more comfortable in tailored suits, and if she wasn't at work, she was wearing sweatpants or cargo shorts and T-shirts.

"But why for so long?" she asked as she joined Vanessa on the couch. "You know as well as I do that Vera's planning everything the way *she* wants it to be, so I don't understand why you even need to be there other than for the ceremony."

"I need to give my opinion on things."

"Even if she won't listen to anything you say? This is going to be an event for her and her social circle. How many people have you actually invited that *you* really want to be there?"

"I don't have a lot of friends, you know that. And neither do you since you brought it up." Vanessa smiled to show she didn't mean anything negative by her words, but even if she did, it wouldn't have mattered to Vic. She was fine without any more than a couple of close friends. Vanessa leaned forward to look her in the eye. "I love you for agreeing to be there with me. It means more than you know. But can we put the animosity for Mother away for the next three weeks? Please?"

Vic shook her head and gave a small smile. "I'll try, but if she pushes me, you know I'll push back."

"Understood, and I wouldn't expect anything less." Vanessa got to her feet and headed for the door. She stopped when she reached it and looked over her shoulder. "We're going in your car, right?"

"Yeah," Vic said as she stood and faced her. Vanessa had come a long way since the accident, but she was still wary about driving. Vic really couldn't blame her. No doubt she'd be reluctant to get behind the wheel too if it had happened to her. "Just be ready to leave first thing in the morning."

"I'll be ready."

Vic went back to the window and stared at the skyline. Truth be told, facing Vera again didn't worry her in the least. The possibility of running into Riley Warren was what had her stomach all tied up in knots. She tilted her head back and closed her eyes. Riley was her greatest regret in life. She'd played a part in making Riley's life a living hell their senior year, and it had torn her apart for the past twenty years.

She let out a breath and shook her head. If only she'd had the guts back then to admit she'd been in love with Riley, her life might have turned out completely different. Then again, maybe things had turned out exactly as they were meant to. Living a life devoid of true feelings for another human being must have been her penance for being an asshole in high school.

"Knock, knock," her father said as he stuck his head into her office. "I really did knock, but you must not have heard me."

"Sorry, I was lost in thought." She smiled and motioned for him to come in. She took a seat behind her desk as he sat across from her. "What's up?"

"I hope your thoughts were good ones."

"Not really." She crossed her arms over her chest and leaned back.

"I know you aren't happy about going back home," he said with a look of sympathy. "And I can't really blame you. Your mother's never been one to give up on a grudge."

"I didn't come out to piss her off, you know. I did it because I needed to be true to myself. She thinks everything is about her, and I just don't understand it, Dad."

"I know, honey," he said with a shrug. "I have to admit I don't totally understand it myself. She wasn't always like this."

"That's good to hear," Vic said. "I'd like to think you have better taste than to get involved with someone who has the personality of a paper bag."

"Hey," he said, trying to look stern but not really accomplishing it. "She's still my wife, you know."

"But you can change that," Vic said with a wink. "Unfortunately, she's always going to be the woman who gave birth to me. Even if she refuses to call me her daughter."

"If it makes you feel any better, she isn't any happier than you are that you'll be staying at the house for the next few weeks."

"Yeah, about that," Vic said as she tilted her head to the side. "I can't believe she'd allow me under her roof again just because Vanessa wants me there."

"I want you there too," he said with an affectionate smile. "And it is my house too, you know. I still have some say in what goes on there. Are you going to be able to get along with her?"

"Doubtful, but it will totally be up to her. If she can be civil, so can I." They sat in silence for a few moments, and she struggled with whether or not to tell him about the fact she was seriously considering leaving the Thayer Group. She decided it could wait. The next three weeks were about Vanessa and her special day, even if Vera would no doubt do everything in her power to make it about herself.

"So, you're going up there tomorrow?" he asked.

"Leaving in the morning."

"I'll see you up there then." He stood and looked at her. "You have everything covered while you're gone?"

"There was only one meeting that couldn't be rescheduled, and Jim is taking care of it for me," she said about her vice president of marketing. "Everything's good."

"Wonderful. Drive safely, okay?"

"I always do." She watched him leave and glanced at the clock. Only ten more minutes left in her day, and then tomorrow she'd be back in Wolf Bay for the first time in sixteen years.

She just hoped to God she could make it through the next three weeks without strangling someone. Or, more accurately, without strangling Vera.

CHAPTER TWO

Wolf Bay, New York, was a nice enough town, but Riley couldn't figure out for the life of her why anyone would actually *want* to live here. Or, for that matter, why it was even called Wolf Bay in the first place. The closest body of water was the Hudson River, and it was an hour away. They were literally closer to the Connecticut state line.

Of course, *she'd* spent her whole life in this town, but she hadn't been given much of a choice in the matter. If she'd had money she could have moved away, but managing a two-screen movie theater in a town of less than eight hundred people wasn't going to get her the money she needed to improve her lot in life.

Owning that theater though, could give her the money she never had. Not *Thayer* money of course, but if she could ever manage to keep over a hundred dollars in her bank account in any given month, she might be able to breathe a little easier. The place did a better than average business thanks to the surrounding small towns and their limited choices for entertainment unless they wanted to drive over an hour away to Albany. But she wasn't naive enough to think she'd ever manage to save enough money to buy it. The owner was willing to sell, but he was asking for more money than she would ever see in her lifetime.

But hey, at least she wasn't living in the rundown trailer park she'd grown up in and where her mother still resided. Her mother's dreams had died long ago, when she'd first decided to find solace in the bottom of a liquor bottle. It didn't much matter to her what kind of liquor it was, just so long as the end result was passing out and forgetting all of her problems. And that seemed to happen pretty much on the daily.

Riley tore her eyes away from the view out the kitchen window of the home she shared with Megan and looked down at the scars on her right arm. She'd been burned worse than she thought the night she saved Vanessa Thayer's life, but an entire year later, she was fully healed and doing fine. Well, except for the scars. At first she'd tried to keep them covered to stop the questions and pitying looks, but she didn't care anymore. It was too damn hot in upstate New York during the summer to wear long sleeves.

She looked at the newspaper next to her arm and sighed. Vanessa Thayer was getting married at her family's estate in three weeks, and the entire town was abuzz about the event. Riley wanted to gag. All she remembered of Vanessa from high school was what a colossal bitch she'd been. It seemed as though her entire existence revolved around how many people she could hurt. And during their senior year, her sights had been set on Riley and her very small circle of friends. She'd succeeded in making Riley's life a living hell. So much so that Riley had even contemplated killing herself. For about a minute.

Megan was the one who talked her out of it by pointing out Vanessa Thayer wasn't worth it. By killing herself, Riley would be letting her win, and there was no way Riley ever wanted *that* to happen. She leaned back and let out a breath as she ran her fingers through her hair.

Not that Vanessa's twin sister, Victoria, had been much better. They'd been sort of friends up until high school, and sure, she'd tried to stand up for Riley occasionally, but it always seemed half-hearted at best. She'd run with the same crowd as her sister and had done her fair share of bullying too. Unfortunately, that hadn't changed the fact Riley had always had a huge crush on Vic.

"Mail call," Megan said as she walked in the front door. She tossed the mail on the table and took a seat across from Riley. "You're ready for the reunion Saturday night, right? You scheduled someone else to work?"

"I did, but I really don't want to go."

"Come on, we've gone to every one they've had." Megan pushed out her lower lip and batted her eyes, causing Riley to chuckle. "You do this every time, you know. And you always end up going, so just stop complaining about it."

"I just read in the paper that Vic and Vanessa are going to be in town," Riley said, turning the paper so it was facing Megan. "What if they show up there? I really don't want to see either of them ever again."

"Oh, please," Megan said with a wave of her hand. "They've never attended a reunion, and they're both big shots in New York City running their family empire. What makes you think they would lower themselves to be seen mingling with the residents of Wolf Bay? Besides, I'm sure you wouldn't *really* mind seeing Victoria again, am I right?"

Riley shook her head and rolled her eyes at the way Megan waggled her eyebrows. She wished she'd never admitted to her in high school how she felt about Victoria Thayer. Most people would have probably forgotten all about it after twenty years, but no, not Megan.

"Fine, I'll go," Riley said, knowing the choice was never in doubt. She hadn't had many friends in high school, but Peter came from California for every reunion they'd had, and she always loved seeing him again. As did Megan, which is why she was so adamant they had to go.

"You saved Vanessa's life," Megan said, as if that meant something. "That should give you brownie points with them, don't you think?"

Riley nodded, because she'd certainly thought so, but she'd never gotten so much as an acknowledgment from anyone in the Thayer family for what she'd done. Not that she'd expected—or even wanted—anything from them, but a simple thank you would have been nice.

"You said yourself they wouldn't want to associate with anyone from Wolf Bay, so does it really surprise you they wouldn't concede anyone from here would do anything to help them?" Riley sighed and got to her feet. "But I'm over it. And if they do show up for the reunion, I will never forgive you."

Megan blew her a kiss, knowing as well as Riley did she'd never stay mad at her for anything. She grabbed her backpack and headed for the door.

"Have a nice night at work, Riley," Megan called out. "Love you."

"Love you too," she replied before walking out of the house they shared. She'd be lying if she said she didn't find Megan attractive, but Megan was as straight as they come. They were too good as friends to mess it up by sleeping together anyway. Megan was the sister she never had, and honestly? Riley didn't know what she'd have done if they hadn't become friends back in junior high. No doubt she would have ended up just like her mother. That thought sent a shiver through her body.

Twenty minutes later, she was sitting in her office making up the employee schedule for the following week. All of her employees, other than her two assistant managers, were high school students. They were all good kids and never gave her a bit of trouble. She tried to accommodate their requests for days off as much as she could, and in return they were always on time and hardly ever stood around doing nothing.

Sure, they occasionally had friends stop by, but they were pretty good about limiting the visits to around five minutes, and as far as she could tell, they weren't giving away concessions or letting their friends in for free. The one time she did catch someone doing those things, they were fired immediately, and the remaining employees knew beyond a shadow of a doubt what would happen if they tried the same thing.

She posted the schedule outside her office door and then sent in her weekly order for supplies before heading out to make sure the concession stand was well stocked for the next show.

"Hey, boss," said Nancy, an assistant manager and the only person working for her who was older than Riley. The woman was perpetually cheery, and there were days it grated on Riley's nerves. Most of the time though, it helped to bring Riley out of whatever funk she happened to be in. Today was one of those days. "It's a beautiful day, isn't it?"

"It is," Riley replied with a nod as she glanced toward the front doors. It was the beginning of June, and they'd soon be open for show times all day every day rather than the abbreviated schedule of evenings only during the week while school was in session. "Summer's almost here."

"Hooray!"

Riley smiled and shook her head. To her, summer merely meant she'd have to deal with kids at the theater all day long. Not really high on her list of favorite things. She would think that every spring, but then it never turned out as bad as she expected it to be.

Nancy and her husband, Andy, had been good friends to her not only when she was younger, but also now. She usually went to their house to play board games at least once a week, and they hosted poker games at their house once a month. Riley's mother had worked with Andy, back when she was able to function without a shot of something in her system, so when she started to drink regularly, Andy and Nancy had taken it upon themselves to look after Riley the best they could.

She shuddered to think about what her life might have been if not for them.

CHAPTER THREE

R iley was sitting at her desk later that evening, entering the inventory and ticket sales for the previous show, when her cell phone rang. She grabbed it without looking to see who it was and held it between her shoulder and ear before going right back to what she was doing.

"Hello."

"Riley, we just dropped your mother off at Marshall Memorial."

Riley nearly dropped the phone when the words Megan said registered in her mind. She felt her heart rate speed up and she sat back in the chair. The hospital was two towns over and a good thirty-minute drive, and she knew before Megan even continued what she was going to say.

"She's in the ER now, and I have to be honest with you, it doesn't look good."

"What happened?" Riley didn't really care, and she knew that probably made her a horrible person. But in all honesty, Helen Warren had never been a good mother. Hell, she'd never even been an okay mother. She'd never paid any attention to Riley, unless it was to yell at her for some asinine reason. Riley had been neglected most of her childhood, but mostly she was subjected to nonstop verbal abuse on a daily basis.

"Alcohol poisoning," Megan said. "I really think you should get to the hospital."

"Is she conscious?"

"Off and on. She had two seizures in the ambulance on the way. We picked her up at that dive bar in Summerville. The bartender called nine-one-one when she fell off a barstool and started seizing."

"Megan, you know I can't just drop everything and rush right over there," she said in spite of the fact she was gathering her things and getting ready to do exactly that.

"Honey, I know deep down you love her even though you bitch about her all the time. No matter what, she's still your mother."

"Fine, I'm leaving now."

"My shift is over in another hour. I'll come back to sit with you."

"Hey, Megan?" Riley said quietly. "Thank you."

She shoved her phone in her pocket and headed out to the concession stand. She spotted Nancy speaking to a customer and hung back to wait for her to finish. When Nancy finally turned to her she took her by the arm and led her a few feet away from everyone else.

"What's wrong?" Nancy asked, obviously seeing it in her face.

"My mom's in the hospital. Megan says it doesn't look good."

"Oh, my God, Riley, you should go," Nancy said, urging her toward the front doors. "Don't worry about us. I'll close everything up."

"Thanks," she said as she gave her a quick hug.

"If you think about it, give me a call and let me know how she's doing. And don't worry about tomorrow either. I'll work so you can stay with her."

Riley waved over her shoulder to let her know she heard, but honestly, she had no intention of taking the next day off. Yes, deep down she did have some love for her mother, but she was pretty sure she wouldn't do much grieving for her when the time came.

There'd been so many nights when she was growing up her mother never even bothered to come home because she was out drinking and picking up men. Riley was left on her own to get her dinner and do her homework, and most of the time to get her own breakfast and off to school on time. When her mother did bother to come home, she criticized everything Riley did. Nothing was ever good enough for her. She never missed an opportunity to tell Riley she'd never amount to anything, and that no one would ever love her.

The worst part though, was when she told her mother about the bullying she was enduring at school and was told she brought it upon herself. It didn't seem to matter most of the bullying was because of the clothes she was forced to buy from Goodwill, and because her mother was an alcoholic.

Riley shook her head to try to get rid of the thoughts, but it didn't do any good. She'd suffered her first panic attack at the age of twelve, and her mother simply told her it was all in her head. She spent most of junior high and high school suffering with anxiety, until her guidance counselor suggested she see a doctor about it. Meds and a lot of therapy helped, and she hadn't had an attack in over fifteen years now.

She pulled into a parking spot near the ER and sat there for a moment, trying to brace herself for what she might face inside. Hopefully, her mother was still unconscious, otherwise she'd probably get an earful about how long it took her to get there. She considered waiting until Megan arrived, but ultimately decided to just suck it up and go inside.

"I'm here for my mother," she said to the woman sitting at the desk as she walked into the ER. "Helen Warren? She was brought in by ambulance."

She didn't have to wait long before a nurse appeared by her side. She escorted her to the bay her mother was in and left her standing inside the drawn curtain just staring at her. She looked so helpless lying there, but Riley was having trouble conjuring up much sympathy for her. Her mother had been heading down this road for years, knowing it would probably kill her someday, but she never seemed to care. Not enough to do anything about it anyway.

She took a seat next to the bed, and after a few minutes her leg began to bounce because she was bored and anxious. Not anxious enough to have an attack, she knew how that felt. Her vision would grow dim and it would be increasingly difficult to breathe. This anxiety was simply because she wanted to be anywhere but here, wondering if her mother would ever wake up.

"Ms. Warren?" a man said as he entered the cubicle. "I'm Dr. Matthews. I'm in charge of your mother's case this evening."

"Hello," she said as she got to her feet and shook his hand. She glanced at her mother before focusing on him. "How is she?"

"I won't lie to you," he said, looking her right in the eye. "She isn't doing well. This isn't her first time here in our ER. Were you aware of that?"

"No." Riley was conflicted. She was caught between being angry her mother hadn't told her and not being at all shocked that she hadn't. "No, I had no idea."

"I'm not surprised. She's made it clear she didn't want anyone to contact you, so I'm wondering how you knew she was here tonight?"

"My best friend is one of the paramedics who brought her in. She called to let me know."

"Okay," he said with a nod before getting her mother's chart from the foot of the bed. "She's been in and out of consciousness even before she arrived in the ER. She's been vomiting, and she's had four seizures. We have her on fluids, as you can see, and she's receiving oxygen through the tube in her throat because she isn't able to keep breathing on her own at the moment. Her stomach was pumped not long after she got here, and there really isn't much else we can do other than monitor her vital signs and wait for the alcohol to vacate her system."

"Will she be okay?"

The doctor didn't say anything right away as he kept his eyes on the chart he was looking at. After a moment he met her eyes again. "I'm optimistic for a full recovery, but there aren't any guarantees. The sooner she wakes up and is able to breathe without assistance the better her chances are."

Riley nodded and sat back down with a sigh. She couldn't shake the feeling that this might be it for her mother. A part of her felt a modicum of relief at the thought, but the little girl she'd never had the opportunity to be felt fear at the thought of never being able to connect with the woman who'd done such a dreadful job of raising her.

"I'll be back in about an hour or so to check on her," the doctor said before exiting.

Riley sat there just watching her mother, wondering if she would wake up. Her head moved a couple of times, and there was a hand twitch, but her eyes never opened. She'd been there for about half an hour when Megan walked in.

"Any change?" she asked as she pulled a chair over and sat next to Riley. Riley just shook her head but didn't look at her. "How are you doing?"

"I'm fine," Riley said.

"What did the doctor say?"

"That they would have to wait and see when she regains consciousness." She sighed before turning her head to look at Megan. "Did you know she's been here before?"

"No," Megan said, and Riley could tell by her expression she was being honest with her. "I would have told you. Why didn't anyone ever call you?"

"Apparently, she told them not to. She doesn't want me here, so why should I stay?" Riley knew she sounded whiny, but she couldn't help it. What kind of mother wouldn't want her daughter to know she was in the hospital?

"Riley?" She whipped her head back toward her mother, who was watching her and Megan. It was almost impossible to understand her with the tube in her throat, but Riley managed somehow. "What are you doing here?"

"I was just wondering the same thing," she said as she got to her feet. Megan left the bay, presumably to notify someone she was awake.

"You should leave." Her mother was still watching her, and she looked angry. "Thank you for coming, but you don't have to stay."

Riley nodded in a daze, but she didn't move. The doctor came in behind Megan. Riley knew he was talking, but she couldn't hear anything he was saying above the pulse pounding in her ears. It was one thing to realize she wasn't wanted there, but quite another to have her mother actually say the words to her. She turned and left, not looking back even when Megan called after her. She was done being stupid by hoping there was some way to mend the relationship with her mother.

It was glaringly obvious her mother had been right when she'd told her no one would ever want her.

Not even the woman who gave birth to her.

CHAPTER FOUR

Haven't seen you here in a while," said Tyler, Vic's best friend, who also happened to be the bartender in her favorite restaurant and bar. He set a coaster down in front of her and smiled. "The usual?"

"Yes, and keep them coming," she said. She watched him as he turned to get the top-shelf bourbon she preferred. He didn't come across as being gay. Most people saw him and thought he was a typical "man's man." He was over six feet tall, and his biceps were almost bigger than Vic's thighs. His hair was blond and a little shaggy, and his eyes a deep blue. He tended to get a lot of attention from the women who came in, and they tipped him well.

"Tough day?" he asked as he set her drink on the coaster.

"I'm just really not looking forward to going back home for the next three weeks."

"I can sympathize," he said with a boyish grin. "I'm going to miss seeing your beautiful face around here."

"I see why you get so many women's phone numbers." She held her glass up in a salute before taking a drink. She closed her eyes against the burn as it went down her throat to settle in her stomach. "You're a relentless flirt."

"I can't help it." He shrugged and wiped a nonexistent dirty spot on the bar. It was Thursday, but the crowds wouldn't come until later, long after Vic was home and probably in bed. "So, you're actually going to be staying with Mommie Dearest?"

"Crazy, right? I just can't say no to Vanessa."

"Well, you know I'm only a phone call away if you need a voice of sanity."

"You may come to regret that offer."

"I'm surprised Vera is allowing you to stay in her house." Tyler shook his head because he knew all about how Vera felt about her. And how she felt about Vera.

"It's only because Vanessa insisted, I'm sure." Vic took another drink before continuing. "If it was up to Vera I wouldn't even be allowed at the wedding, much less spending three weeks under her roof. I'll probably spend a lot of time in the town I wanted so badly to get away from just so I don't have to deal with her any more than absolutely necessary."

"Does *she* still live there?" His emphasis on the word let Vic know exactly who he was referring to. Riley Warren.

"She did a year ago." Vic shrugged. "She's the one who saved Vanessa after her accident."

"Excuse me?" Tyler said, taking a step back and placing a hand over his heart. "You never mentioned that little tidbit before."

"It didn't seem important in the grand scheme of things."

"But you've told me *everything* about her. Why didn't you reach out to her when it happened and try to set things right?"

"I'm ninety-five percent sure she doesn't want anything to do with me or my family." Vic downed the last of her drink and Tyler grabbed the bourbon to refill it.

"But there's always that five percent chance she could surprise you."

"You're such a romantic." Vic laughed at him. "Don't let that get out or you'll have more women after you than ever."

"They can come after me all they want, but they'll never catch me."

"I'm sure all the single men, gay or straight, out there are thankful for that."

"You know it." He waved at a couple at the end of the bar and excused himself to go and wait on them.

God, how she wanted to believe his five percent theory, but she knew better than to hope Riley could possibly have any feelings for her other than contempt and hatred. And she wouldn't blame her one bit after the way she'd been bullied in high school. Vanessa and her friends had been relentless for a few months during their senior year because they assumed she was a lesbian, and even though Vic had tried to get them to stop, she'd ended up joining in because some of them had started to think she might be gay too since she'd been standing up for Riley.

Of course she had been, but she hadn't really been aware of it at the time. She should have been because she wasn't interested in boys at all, but she assumed it was just the boys in Wolf Bay she'd been indifferent toward. She'd hoped college would change things for her, and it most definitely had, but not in the way she'd thought it would.

"Promise me you'll at least try and talk to her," Tyler said when he returned. "You are an awesome woman, and she should be given the chance to get to know you as you are now. Let her know how you always felt about her."

"I can't promise that," she said, shaking her head as she stared at the amber liquid in her glass. "Just the thought of her rejecting me makes my heart hurt."

"Aww, who's the romantic now?"

"Not romantic, just realistic. They all assumed she was a lesbian back then, but I don't know for sure she is. She could be married with a whole house full of kids."

"She could be, but if you spend your entire time there avoiding her, you'll never know, will you?" He walked away to wait on another customer without giving her an opportunity to respond.

It was a nice thought, but Vic knew she wouldn't seek Riley out. She'd spent years building walls to protect her heart, and she knew without a doubt Riley Warren had the ability to break through them all.

She downed half her drink, then stared into the glass again as her mind went back more than two decades to the one day she'd never been able to forget. It was the one moment that haunted her because Vanessa had shocked the hell out of her with the words she'd yelled at Riley.

"Hey, dyke," Frank Mills said with a grin as he grabbed his crotch then rubbed up against Riley's hip. "You just need a good man to show you what you're missing, you know? I could help you with that."

Vic cringed at the words, and she wanted nothing more than to shove Frank against the lockers and castrate him. He was such an ass. She really didn't know what Vanessa saw in him.

"And you really think you're the one who can do that?" Riley asked him as she shoved him away, and Vic silently cheered for her. "When I hear the word 'man,' I can assure you that you are not what comes to mind."

"You fucking bitch," he sneered as he towered over her. "I should kill you."

"Frank, knock it off," Vic said. "You're such an asshole."

"You a dyke too, Victoria?" he said as he turned his attention to her. He grabbed his crotch again and grinned at her. "Maybe you need a little of this."

Vic looked at Vanessa, but she was just laughing at him. The others were all laughing too, and Vic felt her anger beginning to rise. She looked at Riley and saw her pleading with her eyes for Vic to make this stop, but she couldn't. Not if she wanted to keep the peace with this group who had always been tighter with Vanessa than with her.

"You wouldn't be able to handle me, Mills," she said with a forced chuckle. Frank returned his focus to Riley then.

"She isn't worth it, Frankie," Vanessa said. Vic thought she might gag at the nickname.

"Yeah, her mother's a drunk, and I'm pretty sure the shirt she's wearing is one my mother donated to Goodwill last summer. She's a fucking loser and isn't worth the effort, Frank," Harper, Vanessa's best friend, said. "And she's nothing but trailer trash."

"You're all assholes!" Riley yelled at them as she met every one of their eyes. Vic sucked in a breath because she knew standing up to this group just wasn't done.

"Harper's right," Vanessa said, her face turning red with anger. "You're nothing but a loser. Why don't you do us all a favor and just kill yourself?"

They all laughed again, but they turned and walked away from her. Vic stood there for a second, wondering if she should apologize for what Vanessa had said, but she'd been so shocked at the words she couldn't even form a coherent thought. She looked at Riley and hoped she'd see in her eyes how sorry she was before she ran to catch up with the others.

To this day she couldn't believe Vanessa had said it. It almost made her physically ill to think how all their lives might have changed if Riley had taken Vanessa's words to heart and actually done it.

She finished her drink and got to her feet after leaving her money next to the glass, along with a hefty tip, and walked out of the bar. She promised herself right then and there that sometime over the next three weeks, she would talk to Riley and try to make things right.

If that was even possible.

Chapter Five

There was a phone call about an hour ago," Nancy said Friday afternoon, sounding even more low-key than usual. Riley looked at her, wondering what was wrong. Nancy seemed to find straightening boxes of candy more interesting than elaborating on the mysterious phone call.

"Are you going to tell me what it was about, or are you going to make me guess?"

"You'd never guess." Nancy shook her head but met her eyes as she took a deep breath. "They want to have a bachelorette party here."

"Seriously?" Riley finished getting the popcorn machine going and then leaned against the counter and looked at her, her arms folded over her chest. Who the hell wanted to have a bachelorette party in a movie theater? It certainly wouldn't be her first choice of venues.

"Yeah," Nancy said with a chuckle. "And they want to know if you can get *Fifty Shades of Grey* to show for them."

"Wonderful." Riley rolled her eyes but didn't move from her spot. She was sure she could get the film, but did she really want to? A theater full of crazy women who would no doubt be drunk sounded like her worst nightmare. "I assume you have a number for me to call back?"

"Yeah, about that," Nancy said hesitantly.

In that moment Riley's mind went exactly where she didn't want it to go—Vanessa Thayer. But no, it couldn't be her, could it? Why would someone with more money than God want to have her bachelorette party at a movie theater in Wolf Bay? The thoughts went through her mind in the half a second it took Nancy to tell her what she'd been holding back.

"The woman who called was Victoria Thayer." Nancy looked down at her feet after blurting it out, and Riley just stared at her. This could not be happening. Nancy knew all about her crush back in high school, and she also knew the hell Riley had gone through with the group of kids Vic chose to hang out with.

"No," Riley said, her voice quiet. "I won't do it."

"She offered to buy out the theater for twice what you would get if the picture sold out."

"She could pay ten times and never miss the money." Riley knew she was being childish, but she couldn't help it. There was a part of her—a big part, if she was being honest with herself— that simply wasn't able to push the past aside. The other part of her knew rationally that people changed, and twenty years was a long time. But apparently it wasn't *enough* time.

"Honey, I know how you must be feeling, but don't you think you should give her the benefit of the doubt?" Nancy said softly as she placed a hand on Riley's arm. "At least give them the opportunity to try and right some wrongs."

"They had the chance to do that after Vanessa's accident," Riley said, meeting Nancy's eyes and refusing to look away. "It's not like it was a mystery who saved her life that night. Megan made sure of that. My name was in the paper and on the news out of Albany. And not one member of that fucking family even attempted to thank me in any way."

Nancy grimaced at her use of the swear word. She and Andy were devout Christians and they never swore. At least they didn't around Riley. They knew better than to think they could change her, so while they disapproved of the language, they hadn't said a word about it to her in the past twenty years. They'd had plenty of conversations with her about it before she graduated high school though.

"You should at least call her back." Nancy walked away to go to the box office since they were about to start selling tickets to the next show. "She doesn't know you're the manager here. I never gave her your name. But you should be the one to tell her no."

Riley fumed for a moment, but knew Nancy was right. If she was going to refuse to let them have their party here, she needed to be the bearer of the news. She had no right to delegate it to someone else. She picked up the piece of paper containing Vic's number that Nancy had set on the counter on her way past.

"I'll call her tomorrow," she muttered to herself as she shoved the number into her pocket. She really didn't want to deal with her today. She needed time to mentally prepare for talking to Vic again after so many years. She knew it was nothing more than an excuse, and Megan would no doubt give her hell for it, but she didn't care.

As if she'd conjured her up, Riley's phone rang and she saw by the display it was Megan. She chuckled as she answered the call.

"Hi," she said. "Hold on a second." Riley turned to Nancy, who was returning to the concession stand after making sure Tommy was set up with everything he needed in the box office. "Nancy, I have a call. Let me know if it gets too busy and you need me."

"Will do." Nancy waved her off and Riley retreated to the office.

"What's up, Megan?" she asked as she sat at her desk.

"Just wanted to let you know I'm going out with some people for a drink after work. You're welcome to come with us."

"No, thanks," Riley said with a shake of her head even though she knew Megan couldn't see her. "I need some sleep after being at the hospital last night. I'd think you would too since we stayed up all night talking about how awful my mother is."

"What's that saying? We can sleep when we're dead?" Megan laughed. "I won't be out late. I'll try not to wake you up when I come in."

"I'd really appreciate it if you didn't." Riley laughed with her before they said they're good-byes and hung up.

It was busy as usual for a Friday night, but Riley was aware of the phone number burning a hole in her pocket through it all. She was entering all the numbers for the inventory after the last show started when Nancy came into the office and took a seat.

"Everything's all cleaned up and ready for tomorrow?" she asked without looking away from what she was doing.

"Yes, it is. Tommy's out there in case anyone comes out to buy anything," Nancy said, referring to the kid who worked in the box office on weekends. "How's your mother doing?"

Riley sighed but didn't say anything until she was done with her work. Nancy waited patiently for her to respond. After she shut the computer down, she swiveled her chair to face her.

"I don't know," she said with a shrug. "She didn't want me at the hospital. Something she made clear to the staff all the other times she'd been in the ER there and no one ever told me."

"I don't know what that woman is thinking sometimes." Nancy didn't even try to hide her anger. "It was obvious she didn't know what the hell she was doing while you were younger, but I'd hoped she would have gotten better now that you're an adult."

"Yeah, the problem there is she can't get me to do things for her anymore, so she has no use for me." Riley shook her head with a wry smile. "And believe me, the feeling is mutual."

"It just isn't right," Nancy said. "A mother should love her children unconditionally. From what I've seen and heard, she doesn't even know how to love."

"You're right, Nancy, she doesn't. She never has. But you know what? I'm used to it, and it doesn't much bother me anymore."

"I don't believe that. You're saying it didn't bother you when she basically kicked you out of her room last night? No matter how you feel about her, I can't imagine it didn't hurt your feelings at least a little bit."

"It did a little, I won't lie, but it's her. It's just the way she is. The way she's always been," Riley said with a shrug. She hated trying to defend her mother, especially to people who knew her. She decided then and there she wasn't going to do it any longer. Her mother obviously didn't need her any longer, so why should she keep holding out for acceptance? "But you're right. I deserve better. That's why I'm so happy you and Andy are in my life. You've been more like parents to me than she ever was. I really do love you guys, you know that, right?"

"We love you too, Riley," Nancy said. They both stood and hugged tightly. "You're coming for game night on Sunday, right?"

"Wouldn't miss it for the world." Riley smiled as Nancy left the office. She didn't know when her mother was being released from the hospital, and she didn't care. She'd obviously found her own way home from there before, so she wasn't going to put her life on hold wondering if she needed to give her a ride.

Helen Warren was on her own. Much like Riley had been for most of her childhood.

Chapter Six

"We should go to the reunion next weekend," Vanessa said as she and Vic were walking through the gardens at their parents' estate. "It might be fun."

"Fun? Are you nuts?" Vic asked incredulously. She stopped walking and grabbed Vanessa by the wrist to get her to stop as well. "I have absolutely no desire to see any of those idiots we called friends back then. I can just imagine they haven't changed a bit. Have you even talked to any of them since graduation?"

"Just Harper," Vanessa admitted with a shrug. Vic fought the urge to roll her eyes. Harper had been the biggest bitch of the entire group.

Vic led her to the bench a couple of feet away. Vanessa was doing so much better after her accident, but she still had some pain if she tried to overdo things. The burns on her legs had been bad, and she still had trouble walking too far without the use of a cane or walker, which she hated with a passion. The scars were bad enough for Vanessa to never want to be seen in anything other than pants anymore, and Vic knew how hard that was for her fashion plate sister.

At least the accident facilitated her stopping smoking. She'd had a lit cigarette in her hand when it happened, which was the reason for the fire. If not for that, she would have walked away from it with little more than a few broken bones and the eight-inch cut on her forehead from where she'd slammed into the steering wheel.

"Then why would you want to go?"

"Riley," Vanessa said quietly, and sounding more humbled than Vic had ever heard her before.

"Riley?" Vic wasn't able to hide the surprise in her voice. "What about her?"

"Somebody should finally thank her for what she did that night, don't you think?"

"You never did?" Vic stared at her in disbelief. "Jesus, Vanessa, why the hell not?"

"Mother said there was no point," Vanessa said with another shrug. Vic watched as her fingers went to the scar just under her hairline and she massaged it absently. "She thought Riley only did it hoping she'd get some kind of compensation for the deed."

"Are you serious?" Vic was shocked but knew she really shouldn't be. Vera had always been like that. "Even if she had expected something in return, which I really doubt because she probably had no clue who you were when she did it, she still saved your damn life that night. Do you comprehend how huge that is? If she hadn't been there, you would have died in that fire."

"I know," Vanessa said, tears in her eyes. Vic sighed and put an arm around her, pulling her closer so Vanessa rested her head on her shoulder.

Their mother had always cared more about her social standing than she did about her twin daughters. As a result, Vic and Vanessa had been best friends growing up, as well as sisters. And now this? Obviously, she hadn't changed over the years, something Vic would have known if she'd ever visited. Now she was glad she'd stayed away.

Their mother was more than appalled by Vic being a lesbian, and she never missed an opportunity to let it be known. They'd only been there since that morning, and Vic had already heard the snide remarks. So far she'd managed to bite her tongue, but she wasn't sure how much longer she could do it.

"I'd think *you'd* want to see her again too," Vanessa said, poking her playfully in the ribs. Vic didn't have to see her face to know she was smiling.

"I would, but I know she probably hates us both." Vic closed her eyes and Riley's face popped into her mind. She wondered what she looked like now. Was she still as hauntingly beautiful as she had been in high school? "The way we treated her is the biggest regret I have in my life."

"Really?" Vanessa sat up straighter and looked her in the eye. "What about not telling her how you felt?"

"You know as well as I do I wasn't completely sure how I felt about her back then." Vic shook her head and leaned forward, her forearms resting on her thighs. Actually, that was a lie because she had known on some level but never wanted to admit it to anyone. Not even to Vanessa, at least not until after she'd been ready to come out. "All I knew for sure was she confused the hell out of me. I didn't even know being with girls was a real option until we went to college."

"I guess you got more of an education than I did, huh?" Vanessa laughed and put a hand on Vic's knee, squeezing gently.

"You can say that again."

"So, can we go?" Vanessa asked. "To the reunion?"

Vic knew she should say no, but the truth was, she really did want to see Riley again. What were the chances she'd forgotten all about high school and moved on? She allowed herself a small fantasy of Riley professing she felt the same way about her.

"I'm here for your wedding, isn't that enough?"

"No." Vanessa smiled at her, and Vic knew she'd agree to anything she wanted. It was how she'd always been. Unable to resist her sister, which was why she'd even hung out with those losers in high school in the first place. And why she was here, at the family estate, now. Anything to make Vanessa happy.

"Fine, we can go," Vic said before standing and holding a hand out to help her up. "Don't say I never did anything for you."

"Just think how much it would piss Vera off if you actually started dating Riley." Vanessa grinned and bumped her shoulder into Vic's.

Vic couldn't help but laugh at the thought, because it certainly would piss her off. Their mother had always referred to Riley and her friends as trailer trash, whether they'd lived in trailers or not. It had always irked Vic, but she'd never said anything about it. God, how she would love to have the opportunity to put Vera in her place.

"Are you just going to sit there staring at your phone, or are you going to actually call her?" Megan asked the next afternoon. Riley was beginning to regret having told her about Vic's request. Megan held her hand out and snapped her fingers. "Give me her number and I'll call."

Riley sighed and entered the number into her phone. She hesitated before actually pressing the call button though, because she had a really bad feeling about this. She put on a good show in letting everyone think she didn't want to talk to Vic because she was pissed about high school. If she was being honest with herself though, she was really afraid of being made to feel like a victim again which was what she knew would happen as soon as she heard Vic's voice. She closed her eyes and gave herself a mental shake. *You can do this.*

She opened her eyes and pressed the button but stared straight ahead. It was bad enough Megan was standing there watching and listening. She didn't need to see whatever faces she decided to make in an attempt to distract her. It rang three times and she was about to hang up before it went to voice mail, but then she answered.

"Victoria Thayer," she said, very businesslike.

Riley opened her mouth, but nothing came out. Her throat constricted and all she could hear for a moment was the blood pulsing in her ears. She knew she must have looked like a deer in headlights as she glanced at Megan, who was giving her a thumbs-up.

"Hello?" Vic said, sounding irritated now. "Who is this?"

"Yes, hello, I'm sorry," Riley said and then cleared her throat. "I'm the manager of the movie theater in Wolf Bay. I had a message you called about a bachelorette party."

"Oh, yes, I did. I'm sorry, but I didn't catch your name."

"My name is Riley Warren," she said before she could change her mind. It gave her a small amount of satisfaction when there was a lengthy pause from the other end of the line. "Ms. Thayer? Are you still there?"

"Riley?" she asked, her voice quiet, and if Riley wasn't mistaken, a little strained. "From Wolf Bay High? Class of two thousand?"

"Yes, that's me." Riley took a long drink from the glass of water Megan handed her before sitting across from her at the kitchen table. When she put the glass back down, Megan reached across and placed a hand on her arm.

"How have you been?"

The question stunned Riley, because who the hell did Vic think she was acting as though they'd been friends?

"A lot better than I was in high school, but why are you asking me that like we're just old friends reconnecting?" Riley pulled her arm away from Megan and stood before beginning to pace. She pinched the bridge of her nose between her thumb and forefinger as she let out a breath. "Because we were anything but friends, Victoria. Or maybe you've conveniently forgotten about that."

"I haven't, Riley, but I wish I could go back in time and change it all. I swear to you I am not that person anymore. I'm so sorry for all of it."

Riley sat back down with a thud, because she sure as hell hadn't been expecting that. She'd spent so many long years feeling nothing but anger and hatred toward the entire Thayer family, and now she gets an apology right off the bat? What the actual fuck?

"Riley?" Victoria asked, a hint of levity in her voice. "Are *you* still there?"

"Yeah," she replied. "So, the reason I'm calling is to tell you I can't let you book the theater for your party."

"Why not? Did the woman I spoke to give you the whole message? I'll pay twice what you'd get if you sold out the theater."

"It's not about the money," Riley said, even though it was a little bit. When she rented out the theater for private parties, or school field trips, the owner let her keep half the money for her trouble of having to deal with what was almost always inevitable headaches.

"Can you not get the film I requested? I'm sure Vanessa has a digital copy of it because it's her favorite movie."

"Okay, slow down. First of all, I'm pretty sure it doesn't work that way, and second, we aren't a big city multiplex. We aren't digital, although we are working on it. We still run movies on actual film through a real projector. And yes, I could probably get the movie you requested."

"Then why are you turning me down?"

"Honestly? I'm not comfortable having anything to do with you or your sister." Riley stared at Megan, who was doing her own version of a happy dance right there in her chair.

"I see." Instead of sounding angry, Victoria sounded almost sad. And Riley hated that she almost felt bad for saying what she did. But what the hell? It was the truth. "Okay, then. Will you allow me the opportunity to show you I've changed?"

"I'm not really sure—"

"Meet me somewhere for coffee. I'd really like to talk to you."

"I can't. I have to work tonight."

"Then tomorrow morning."

Riley moved the phone away from her ear and held it out to Megan who backed away and shook her head.

"She wants to have coffee," Riley whispered.

"Do it," Megan mouthed back. Riley shook her head, not because she didn't want to, but because she couldn't believe any of this was actually happening. Before Victoria thought she'd fallen off her chair, she put the phone back to her ear.

"Fine. Wolf Bay Diner at ten?"

"I'll be there," Victoria said, sounding relieved. "And thank you, Riley. I'll see you in the morning."

The call disconnected and Riley dropped her phone on the table in front of her. She and Megan looked at each other in silence for a moment before Riley groaned and rested her head next to her phone.

"You are a fucking rock star," Megan said before bursting out laughing. "I can't believe you said you weren't comfortable having anything to do with her or her sister. You're awesome!"

"Then why do I feel like I'm going to throw up?"

"Because she was your first crush. Come on, we have to find you something to wear."

Riley groaned louder but got to her feet to follow Megan to her bedroom. She already knew she had next to nothing but jeans and T-shirts or her work uniforms, so if Megan thought something dressier was going to magically appear in her closet, she was sadly mistaken.

Christ, why couldn't she just wear what she usually wore? It wasn't like this was a date or anything. She snorted, causing Megan to stop and turn to look at her. She shrugged. Even if by some miracle Victoria was a lesbian, she'd never look twice at her no matter what she was wearing.

CHAPTER SEVEN

W hat in the world are you wearing?" Vera asked, looking at Vic with utter disdain as she entered the living room. "The least you could do while you're staying in *my* house is dress like a proper woman."

"It's a woman's suit, Vera," she said, thinking she looked damn good if she did say so herself. She took a seat on the sofa and rested her right ankle on her left knee, knowing the move would piss her off even more. "By *Armani*. I thought that would perhaps appease you."

"Couldn't you wear a skirt instead of pants?"

"And miss this reaction?" Vic laughed. "Not on your life. And I don't do skirts, or dresses for that matter. You know this about me."

"You'll be wearing a dress for your sister's wedding." Vera looked smug, and Vic wanted nothing more than to slap it off her face.

"Oh, she didn't tell you?" Vic asked, thoroughly enjoying the way her mother's face fell at the ominous tone of her voice. Vic smiled. "Vanessa found a perfect suit for me to wear that matches the groomsmen."

"No, that most definitely is not acceptable," her mother said, shaking her head and standing. "I'll just have to have a talk with her."

"Vera, let it go," Vic said, her voice raised. "You tried so hard to make me into the woman you always thought I should be, and it didn't change who I am. I'm almost forty years old, and you don't get to dictate what clothes I wear. Wearing a dress for my sister's wedding isn't going to miraculously make me straight."

"What's going on in here?" her father asked as he walked into the room and looked back and forth between them. "I could hear you shouting all the way upstairs."

"You need to have a talk with your daughter."

"*My* daughter? Vera, she's your child too, and it might do you a world of good to at least try and get along with her."

"She comes here for the first time in sixteen years and has the audacity to dress like this in my presence? Perhaps she's the one who should try and get along with *me*."

Vic sat there in silence watching them. Her father's face was turning red with the effort of trying not to yell at Vera, and Vera had the most pained expression on her face, as though Vic being a lesbian was literally going to kill her.

"Is it any wonder she hasn't come home in so long?"

"Garret, are you condoning her behavior?"

"What I'm doing is supporting *our* daughter. She's a wonderful woman, which is something you'd realize if you'd get off your high horse long enough to make an attempt to get to know her. So what if *her* wedding day would have two brides instead of a bride and a groom? Our job isn't to criticize and judge our children, but to love and support them unconditionally."

"I can't believe you'd take her side over mine. Don't you care what people think?"

"Honestly? I couldn't care less what anyone thinks."

"Not even your own wife," her mother said before turning and stomping out of the room.

Vic smiled at her father as he shook his head and came to sit next to her on the couch. Her heart swelled with the love she felt for him for standing up for her.

"That woman could try the patience of a saint," he said after a moment.

"I don't know how you put up with her," Vic said, immediately wishing she hadn't said something negative about Vera. She held her breath for him to turn around and defend Vera.

"Sometimes I don't know either," he said with a chuckle. He turned his head and looked her over. "You're dressed up. Going out tonight?"

"I was thinking about going to see someone I went to school with." Vic hoped Riley wouldn't be pissed at her for just showing up at the movie theater, but after talking on the phone earlier, she didn't want to wait until tomorrow morning to see her. "Someone I wish I'd known better when we younger."

"Oh? A woman?"

"Yes, Riley Warren. Do you know her?"

"Can't say that I really know anyone in Wolf Bay," he said. He actually looked sad at the admission, and Vic wondered if it was simply because of her mother's disdain for the "common" people. If not for her, would he be a man who cared more for his fellow townspeople? "But the name does sound vaguely familiar."

"Mother used to call her trailer trash." Vic felt a slight pain in her chest at the words and assumed it was regret. Regret for not speaking up against the things her mother said, and certainly regret for her younger self having been so small-minded to simply follow the crowd.

"Ah, yes, I remember. Her mother was an alcoholic, right?"

"Yes."

"You should go see her," he said with a nod. "And I hope you get to know her better now. Maybe you could bring her to Vanessa's wedding."

"Yeah, I'm not sure that would ever happen. Not to mention the conniption fit Mother would have if I showed up with a woman on my arm." The visual was rather appealing though, she had to admit. "Especially if it was Riley."

"Don't worry about her," he told her. "If you want to bring Riley, then you absolutely should."

Vic smiled and nodded, wondering if it could ever really be that easy where her mother was concerned. Maybe she'd try to convince Riley to go if she didn't hate her too much.

❖

Riley was threading the film through the projector for the next show when the radio on her hip came to life.

"Riley, there's someone here to see you," said Tommy, who was working the box office.

"I'll be down in a minute," she replied. No one ever came to see her while she was at work other than Megan. It was Saturday, so she hoped it wouldn't be so busy that she couldn't take a few minutes to chat. She quickly finished getting the film ready so all she had to do was press the start button when it was time, then headed down to the lobby. She glanced at the people in the lobby, but didn't see Megan anywhere so she headed toward the box office. "Where's Megan?"

"Oh, it isn't Megan," Tommy said. "I've never seen this woman before."

Dear God, please don't let it be my mother. As soon as the thought crossed her mind, she rejected it. She was no doubt still in the hospital, and even if she wasn't, it was almost nine. If she had been released, there was no doubt in Riley's mind her mother would already be passed out on her couch. She stood there for a moment before looking through the lobby again. She saw a woman dressed in an expensive looking suit leaning against the wall near the concession stand, but a cursory glance told Riley she didn't know her.

Wait just a minute.

The words echoed in her head just as she flicked her eyes away, and she looked back at the woman's face. Her heart seemed to skip a beat when she realized the woman staring back at her was Victoria Thayer. Twenty years had gone by since she'd laid eyes on her, but there was no doubt it was her, even though her hair was much shorter, and she seemed a lot less feminine than she had the last time she saw her. Riley began to walk slowly toward her as Vic's smile widened. When she pushed off the wall, Riley felt a fluttering low in her belly.

"What are you doing here?" she asked, hoping her immediate arousal wasn't obvious. And what the hell? She'd never had such an immediate reaction to a woman before.

"I wanted to see you."

"Yeah, and we arranged to have coffee in the morning." Riley looked around. There were customers, but not so many her employees couldn't handle things without her for a few minutes. "I'm working."

"What time are you done?"

"Not until midnight."

"I'll wait." Vic smiled and pulled some money out of her pocket. "I'll watch the movie and then wait outside for you."

"You do recall me saying I wasn't comfortable having anything to do with you, right?" Riley said as Vic headed toward the doors that would lead her outside and to the box office.

"I do," she answered with a quick nod and another smile. "And it's my intention to change your mind about that."

Riley just stared at her for a moment, not quite knowing what to say. It didn't matter though, because Vic was gone. For now. Christ, she was going to have to be alone with her later. She looked at her watch and saw it was time to start the last show in theater one, so she turned and headed up the stairs. After starting the projector, she pulled out her phone and called Megan.

"Hey there," Megan said.

"Fuck me, she's here. What do I do?"

"Okay, slow down," Megan said. "Who's there?"

Riley took a moment to calm her racing heart. She really hadn't expected such a visceral reaction to seeing Vic again. Who knew her body was such a traitor?

"Vic. She's here, watching the last show, and then she said she's going to wait outside for me to be done with work."

"How does she look?"

"What the hell does that matter?" Riley fought to keep her voice down as she headed for her office behind the concession stand. She had ten minutes before the next movie had to start, but on her way to the office she stopped and asked Nancy to take care of it for her.

"It matters, trust me," Megan said with a slight chuckle. "Did she get fat? Please tell me she's as big as a moose."

"She's not," Riley said, smiling in spite of her anxiety. "She didn't get fat, she didn't get ugly, although she did get a little bit queer."

"And what does that mean, exactly?"

"It means if I were seeing her for the first time, I'd bet my life she was a lesbian."

"Ooh, that's an interesting turn of events, isn't it?" Megan was smiling—Riley could hear it in her voice. "Tell me why you think that."

"All the stereotypical reasons, the hair, the clothes, no purse or makeup, but the real reasons? It's the way she was looking at me, and the way she carries herself." Riley closed her eyes and pictured Vic leaning against the wall. Her stomach did that weird fluttering thing again. "God, Megan, I'm in so much trouble."

"I can stay at Laura's house tonight if you think you might be bringing her home with you," Megan offered, speaking about her older sister. "I wouldn't want to be a third wheel."

"I'm not bringing her home," Riley said, although the thought was more than tempting. She shook her head. "Nope. Not happening."

"Are you trying to convince me or yourself?"

"I'm not sure."

"Well, the offer stands. For whenever you want to bring her home, all right? And I won't wait up for you."

"Thanks, but I called for some advice, Megan. What the hell am I going to do?"

"Talk to her," Megan said, sounding as though it was the most obvious answer in the world. "What's the worst that could happen? You might find out she's still a shallow little harlot and then you can brush her aside and move on."

"That's why I love you, Megan, you're always the voice of reason."

"Of course I am. It's about time you finally figured that out."

She placed her phone on her desk after disconnecting the call and just stared at it. How was it possible for Vic to still have the power to tie her stomach in knots? She'd been so sure that was a purely adolescent phenomenon.

Yeah, she'd been so wrong about that.

CHAPTER EIGHT

Vic waited until the credits were done rolling before getting to her feet. Not because she wanted to see what company had catered the film, but because she was nervous as hell about seeing Riley again. God, how was it possible Riley was even more attractive than she remembered? Even in her nondescript work uniform. Maroon looked good on her. With a sigh, she walked slowly out of the theater and into the lobby. She was about to walk out the doors when she heard her name.

"Victoria," Riley said from a few feet away.

She turned and their eyes met, and her heart rate immediately increased. Her mouth was dry and she couldn't do anything but stare. Riley motioned for her to follow but then stopped and talked for a moment to an older woman Vic didn't recognize. Once the woman nodded at her, Riley motioned her along again. She followed her into an office situated behind the snack bar and took the seat Riley indicated.

"There's no reason you should have to wait outside." Riley sat and began entering numbers into a computer program. Vic figured it was probably inventory counts. She wasn't sure how long she sat there staring at Riley, but when Riley looked at her she felt her cheeks flush. "Victoria?"

"I prefer to be called Vic," she somehow managed to say. She'd always hated her name, mostly because her mother said it was a good feminine name. Vic had never felt feminine a day in her life, not even when she'd dressed the part in her youth. She was finally comfortable enough in her own skin to be herself around Vera, and Vic was the name she preferred.

"Okay," Riley said, sounding somewhat amused. She didn't immediately turn away, but instead was looking at her. *All* of her. Like, head to toe. Vic couldn't stop the goose bumps that broke out along her arms because it felt as though Riley was physically touching her.

"Is something wrong?" Vic asked, glancing down at herself. "I didn't spill my dinner on myself, did I?"

Riley smiled and shook her head as her cheeks flushed, and Vic was pleased to have gotten the desired reaction out of her at the comment.

"I'm just a little surprised to see you dressed like this." Riley shrugged but held her gaze.

"Like what?" Vic tilted her head to one side, amused now herself. She knew what Riley was getting at but decided to let it play out.

"Well, you're a Thayer. I thought you'd have a certain standard to uphold."

"God, is that what you think of us?" Vic grimaced and shook her head. "I'll admit, my mother is like that. Arrogant, overbearing, condescending, self-important. I could go on. And on. Vanessa used to be like that, but not so much anymore. And my father? He's pretty awesome, actually." She met Riley's eyes and held them, wanting to make sure she saw the truth of what she was saying. "I am *nothing* like my mother."

"You used to be. Back in high school."

Vic nodded, because she knew it was true. She felt her face heat with embarrassment. She put that part of herself to rest a long time ago, but Riley wouldn't—couldn't—possibly know that about her. She needed to show her, and not simply tell her. And that was exactly what she intended to do.

"I know I was, and all I can say is I'm sorry," Vic said, feeling her eyes filling with tears. She blinked in an attempt to keep them from falling. "I'm sorry for everything. I completely understand why you would want nothing to do with me, but I'm hoping I can change your mind."

"Why?" Riley asked, looking totally perplexed. "Why would you care what I think of you or your family?"

Vic wasn't sure how to answer that. Back in high school, they'd all been convinced Riley Warren was a lesbian. Now? She was second-guessing herself. She could very well make a fool out of herself if she were to come right out and confess she'd had a crush on her. That she thought even now Riley was the most beautiful woman she'd ever laid eyes on.

"Because I'm not like them," Vic said after a moment. "And because of that, I care what people think of me, to a point."

Riley nodded and turned back to her work. Vic watched for a moment, waiting to see if she'd talk more, but it appeared as though she had no intention of doing anything other than working. Vic's curiosity got the better of her.

"Can I ask you a question?"

"Sure." Riley didn't even look at her.

"What's wrong with the way I'm dressed?"

Riley's breath caught in her throat, but she didn't look at Vic. She couldn't. She didn't want her to see the way her cheeks flushed. She cleared her throat and tried to gather her thoughts. After a few moments of silence, she finally turned in her chair and faced her, unable to keep her eyes from roaming over Victoria's body.

"No offense," she said and then cleared her throat again because her voice cracked. "But dressed like you are, people might assume you're a lesbian."

"Really?" Vic laughed, and the rich tenor of it caused Riley's skin to tingle. "Is that what you think, Riley?"

"Victoria," she said, shaking her head and not having a clue how to respond.

"God, I hate that name. Please, call me Vic." She smiled at Riley. "And I'll respond to you the same way I do my mother. I dress for comfort, and since *I am* a lesbian, why would I care if people think that?"

Riley was taking a drink of water when she heard those words, and she ended up spewing it all over her computer screen and keyboard. She quickly mopped up what she could and looked at Vic, who was laughing again. Riley couldn't help it. She began to laugh too.

"Did you know you were back in high school?" Riley asked once the laughter subsided.

"God, no," Vic said. "I mean, I knew I was different, and of course I knew lesbians existed, but I never knew it could be an option for me, mostly because of my mother. From a young age, it was drummed into our heads that someday we'd find nice men and get married and have lots of children. Obviously, that didn't work out quite as she planned since we're thirty-eight, and this is going to be Vanessa's first marriage."

"So, when did you know?"

"College. Stereotypical, I know, but I was finally away from home and living on my own for the first time, and it was like a whole new world opened up for me." Vic's eyes never strayed from hers, and it was beginning to make Riley a little uncomfortable. "When did you know?"

"Seventh grade," Riley said without even having to think about it. "Miss Miller."

"Really?" She seemed surprised, but then looked as if she were almost contemplative. She nodded after a moment. "Yes, I can understand now that I'm older and able to look back on it. She certainly was attractive."

Riley let out a nervous laugh and looked away from her. She had a horrible thought pop into her mind, and she didn't want

Vic to see it in her expression. She blamed it on having spent too many years dealing with her and her friends bullying her, but she couldn't shake it.

"What's wrong?" Vic asked, sounding concerned.

"How do I know you aren't here telling me these things, getting me to open up about my life, just to turn around and tell all those idiots you hung out with in high school that they were right? Riley's a big old dyke. Let the harassment continue."

"God, we really fucked with your head, didn't we?" Vic's voice sounded strangled, causing Riley to look at her again. She saw the tears in her eyes. Vic shook her head and glanced down at her hands. "I'm so sorry, Riley. I swear to you I would never do that. I'd hope you'd believe me, but of course, you have every reason to doubt it. I would also hope you might remember I did try to stand up for you a few times."

"Half-heartedly at best," Riley choked out. "Most of the time you joined in on it."

"You're right. I won't make excuses, and I won't keep apologizing." Vic stood and began pacing in the small office. "I do want to thank you for something though."

"Oh?" Riley was intrigued. What could she possibly have to thank her for?

"You saved Vanessa's life a year ago. It came to my attention recently that no one in my family bothered to acknowledge the fact." Vic stopped pacing and turned to look at her. "I know how you must feel about her, but she's one of my best friends as well as my sister. So, I want to thank you for what you did that night. It was a wholly unselfish act, and I can see by the scars on your arm that you didn't escape the ordeal unscathed."

Riley looked at her arm, remembering the night it happened as she absently rubbed the scars with her other hand. She hadn't even thought about what she was doing. It was just instinct to help someone in trouble. If she had thought about it at all, she might not have reached into a car that was burning to save the person. It touched her to hear Vic thank her for what she'd done though, and she nodded her thanks.

"How is she after the accident?"

"Her legs were pretty badly burned. She only recently stopped using a cane or walker to help her get around. She'd been in town that night to tell our parents she'd gotten engaged." Vic smiled at some memory Riley wasn't privy to but then shook her head. "He's a good man. He didn't hesitate to rush to her side and took a lot of time off work to help her in her recovery."

"I'm glad she's all right." Riley finished her work and powered down the computer before standing. "I'm done here and need to get home now."

As much as she'd enjoyed chatting with Vic, she was still apprehensive at the motives behind her being there tonight. She wanted to believe the things she was saying, but past experience made her wary.

"Do you have someone waiting for you?" Vic asked. Riley studied her for a moment, wondering why she was asking. Was it possible she was interested in her?

"No." Riley smiled sadly and shook her head.

"I find that hard to believe." Vic followed her out of the theater, and they stopped at the edge of the parking lot. There were only a handful of cars still in the lot, so it wasn't difficult for Riley to determine the Mercedes belonged to Vic.

"Why?" Riley truly wanted to know. Vic looked at her like she was dense.

"Surely you must know how beautiful you are. I thought for sure you'd have settled down and gotten married by now."

"Yeah, right." Riley laughed. "It isn't like Wolf Bay is a hotbed for lesbians. How about you? Do you have a woman waiting for you back in the city?"

"No," she answered with a humorless chuckle. "No time. It seems as though I'm always working."

"That's too bad," Riley said, even though she was inexplicably happy at her answer. "I really should get going. It was nice to see you again."

"Thank you for talking with me." Vic appeared as if she was about to step forward and hug her, but then must have thought better of it. She looked out at the parking lot briefly then back to Riley. "I guess there's no need to meet for coffee in the morning. Unless you'd like to?"

Riley thought about it for a moment, knowing she should say no, but really wanting to say yes. What the hell was wrong with her? She'd never been nervous around a woman before. What was it about Vic that had her feeling this way?

"We could," she said with a one-armed shrug she hoped looked indifferent. "If you want to, that is."

"I do." Vic smiled again and took her keys out of her pocket. "I'll see you in the morning then?"

"Yeah. Good night." Riley watched her walk away and sighed. What was she getting herself into?

CHAPTER NINE

R iley knew when she pulled into the driveway that Megan had waited up for her despite having told her she wouldn't. She smiled because she'd expected this. Megan knew she'd want to talk about her evening.

"I'm disappointed you're home so early," Megan said from her place on the couch when Riley walked in the front door. "I guess things didn't go well."

"As a matter of fact, it did go well. We had a nice chat."

"Really?" Megan looked excited. She sat up straighter and patted the seat next to her. "Tell me all about it."

Riley sat and leaned her head back against the couch as she sighed. It had gone amazingly well, and honestly, the more she reflected on it, the less she thought Vic might be doing this as some colossal joke. She seemed sincere, but Riley's mind was still having trouble reconciling the new Vic with the girl she'd gone to school with.

It was close to one in the morning by the time she finished recounting their conversation, and Megan had sat there, totally captivated by it all. Her smile was so big when Riley finished, she couldn't help but laugh at her.

"Don't laugh," Megan said with a playful slap to her biceps. "You know I'm a total romantic. She sounds interested, don't you think?"

"Why would someone like her be interested in someone like me?"

"The heart wants what the heart wants, Riley." Megan shrugged. "Don't fight it. What would it hurt to see where it goes?"

"My heart wants it, but my head's telling me it's a bad idea all the way around."

"Maybe you should shut your brain off just this once. You once told me you thought the two of you were meant to be together."

Riley snorted and shook her head. "I was sixteen then, for God's sake. I didn't know anything about how life works. I've grown up since then."

"So has she." Megan cocked an eyebrow when Riley looked at her skeptically. "I'm just saying. Maybe she's finally realized what you knew way back when."

"You're so full of shit."

"Just think about it, all right? Seriously. Let it happen. If it wasn't meant to be, then you'll know and you can move on with your boring ass life."

Riley stared at her as Megan got to her feet and walked to her room, closing the door behind her. She closed her eyes and sighed again. Was it really possible Vic could be interested in her? Her heart sped up at the thought, but her mind was screaming at her to slow down and be cautious. She forced her mind to shut down. At least the part that was trying to throw water on the fire she hadn't felt in way too long.

Vic walked into the room she and Vanessa had shared for the first eighteen years of their lives, trying to be quiet so she didn't wake her. For as big as this damn house was, she'd never understood why they always had to share a room. Even now.

Vic would have thought their mother wouldn't want them in the same room. After all, Vic's *lifestyle* could rub off on Vanessa. It surprised Vic their mother had never touched this room in the twenty years since they'd left for college.

She glanced at the desk on her side of the room, and at the locked bottom drawer. What was in that particular drawer would no doubt melt her mother's brain if she'd ever found it. Vic didn't still have the key for it, but she knew how easy it was to get it open with a paper clip, so she sat down and picked the lock. Her heart was pounding as she pulled the drawer open and saw her journal sitting there, right where she'd left it.

After sparing a glance over her shoulder to make sure Vanessa was still asleep, she picked it up and opened it to the middle of their senior year, just as the winter break was beginning. She chose that time because it had been when she started to really consider those confusing feelings about Riley Warren.

God, how she'd wanted to kiss her earlier as they were standing outside the theater. She closed her eyes and let the feelings wash over her. When was the last time she'd ever felt excited about the prospect of seeing someone again? Oh, yeah, it was precisely *never.*

She moved to the bench in the bay window and began reading, thankful the moon was almost full so she didn't have to turn a light on. She smiled at the first mention of Riley's name and ran her fingers over it, remembering.

God, I am so over the way they're treating Riley Warren and her friends. Nobody deserves to be bullied like that. They're so cruel! Riley can't help it if she's poor and has to wear secondhand clothes to school. And as for her mother being a drunk? So not Riley's fault. But what I hate the most is when they call her a dyke and a lesbo. I tried to come to her defense yesterday, but then they just started calling me those names. It bothers me that it bothers me, you know? But then I think, what if I am? I know

I shouldn't give a fuck what anyone thinks of me, but I do care what Vanessa thinks. She's so disgusted by the mere possibility someone in our school might be gay—how would she react if her own twin sister was? So, I can't be a lesbian. But God, Riley confuses the hell out of me. I see her in the halls, and all I want to do is be near her. I sit next to her in English, and all I can think is how good she looks and smells, and I want to be even closer than our desks allow. My heart races, and my palms sweat, and I can't stop thinking about her. I think I want to kiss her, but then I realize kissing her would never be enough. Damn it, I can't wait for graduation, and then I can get out of this shit town and be away from her. Away from the one person I know I'll never be able to have.

Vic looked up when she heard Vanessa stirring. She looked out the window and up at the sky, willing her to not wake up. She closed her eyes against the disappointment when she heard her speak.

"What are you doing?"

"Reading my old journal."

"Jesus, it's…" she paused as she picked up her phone from the bedside table and checked the time, "almost two in the morning."

"I went to see Riley tonight." Vic wished she hadn't spoken the words out loud, because she knew Vanessa would now get up and want to talk.

"She got fat and ugly, didn't she?" She squeezed Vic's shoulder before taking a seat across from her in the window.

"You know damn well she didn't," Vic said, looking at her. Vanessa told her after the accident Riley looked even better now than she had in high school.

"Yeah, well, I was going into shock when I saw her," Vanessa said with a chuckle. "Oh, and my legs were *on fire* at the time, so I don't really know if I can trust what I saw was real."

"It was," Vic assured her, unable to hide her grin. "God, Vanessa, I don't even know how to describe what I felt in her presence."

"Well, you probably shouldn't be too obvious about how you feel in public."

"Why?" Vic looked at her, surprised. Vanessa had always been her greatest champion. Hell, she'd even made sure Martin was cool with her lesbian twin sister before she agreed to a second date. And now she was marrying him.

"You know how Vera is," Vanessa said.

"I don't give a rat's ass how Vera feels about anything."

"I know," Vanessa said, raising her hands in defeat. "And she feels the same way. I hate it that you never come here with me."

"I'm here now, because your wedding is such an important day for you. Any other time, I have no desire to subject myself to Vera's judgmental bullshit." Vic closed the journal and set it aside. She missed spending the holidays with her father and sister, but the animosity with her mother was too much to bear. That, and her mother made it clear she wasn't welcome there. She'd graciously made an exception for Vanessa's wedding. "She still thinks all I need is a good man to show me what I'm missing. You have no idea how much I want to tell her maybe she just needs a good woman to show her what *she's* missing."

"Oh, my God, if you ever do that, make sure I'm in the room." They both laughed at the absurdity of it all. "I wouldn't want to miss her reaction for the world."

"I definitely will." Vic stifled a yawn and stood. "We should probably go to bed before she comes and yells at us for making too much noise."

"I think that may have been her favorite thing to do when we were younger." Vanessa followed suit, and once they were both settled in bed, she spoke again. "Are you going to see Riley again?"

"We're having coffee tomorrow morning," Vic said, smiling even though she knew Vanessa wouldn't be able to see her with the curtains now closed.

"Just be careful, okay? I know Vera doesn't socialize much with the people in town, but I'm sure she has her circle of friends to keep her informed of all the goings on in Wolf Bay."

"You mean the rumor mill? I'm sure she does."

"I'm just looking out for you, you know?" Vanessa asked. "No need to have more stress than you already do."

"I do know, and I appreciate it, Vanessa," she said quietly. "Now I need to get some sleep before I have to deal with her again in the morning. Good night."

"Good night, Vic."

CHAPTER TEN

What the hell are you doing still in bed?" Megan asked, successfully waking Riley from a halfway decent dream. She pulled the covers off her and smacked her hard on the ass. "You're going to be late for your date."

"Go away," Riley muttered, reaching for the sheet only to have her hand batted away.

"Are you listening? You, Victoria Thayer, a date?"

"It's not a date," Riley said as she turned onto her back and looked up at Megan, who was all showered and ready to leave for work. "And I'm not going."

"Yes, it is, and yes, you are." Megan grabbed her by the arm and forced her to sit up. "You'll thank me someday."

"Wouldn't it be just like a Thayer to make plans with me and then stand me up?" Riley asked, her voice a little too whiny to her own ears. "If I don't go, then it won't matter when she doesn't show up."

"Oh, my God, get your pathetic ass out of bed. You're worse than a child sometimes. You're going to go, have coffee and stimulating…conversation…and you're going to enjoy yourself."

"I hate you."

"I know you do, but I love you, so it doesn't matter." Megan went to the door but paused to make sure Riley was really going to get up. "And I want to hear all about it when I get home from work tonight."

"Yes, Mother," Riley said, rummaging through her drawers for something to wear. She figured since Vic had already seen her in her work uniform, it didn't much matter what she wore this morning. She had to know Riley wasn't a fashionista. She glared at Megan as she walked past her on her way to the bathroom. Even though there was a part of her that didn't want to go to the diner, she was grateful Megan had woken her up. She would hate to be the one standing someone up.

When she was done with her shower, she made a quick phone call before rushing out the door. By her estimation, she'd make it to the Wolf Bay Diner just on time.

As she walked into the diner, Amy, the cashier, gave her a small wave. Riley had gone out with Amy once, but never went on a second one. The problem being Amy was about ten years younger than her. Now, maybe that wasn't a big deal to some people, but Riley wanted someone closer to her own age.

Like Vic, who was sitting in a booth toward the back and smiling at her.

Riley took a deep breath and began walking toward her, for some reason unable to look away from Vic. Her blond hair was definitely shorter than it had been in high school. It barely touched her shoulders now. Her bright blue eyes were still the thing that pulled Riley in, but her face had changed the most. Vic had been slightly overweight when she was younger, but her face showed the weight loss while her body definitely displayed Vic's dedication to keeping fit. Riley knew this because of the shorts and tight-fitting T-shirt she wore. When Vic stood to greet her, Riley's heartbeat kicked up a notch.

"I was worried you wouldn't actually come today," Vic said, looking uncharacteristically nervous. At least Riley thought so, because she'd always been so self-assured.

"That's funny," Riley said with a slight smile. "I thought maybe you wouldn't."

A silence that wasn't completely uncomfortable settled over them as they did the awkward hugging thing before sitting down and facing each other across the table. Riley smiled at the waitress who came by to take their orders.

"Feel free to eat if you'd like," Vic told her after ordering just coffee for herself.

"Are you sure?"

"Absolutely."

"In that case, I'll have the special," Riley said to the waitress. "And a coffee, please."

"You look nice," Vic said when they were once again alone. Riley looked down at herself, wondering what looked nice about her faded Yankees T-shirt and cargo shorts.

"So do you," she said, feeling her cheeks grow hot as her eyes landed on Vic's chest briefly. Vic gave her a knowing smile when she snapped her gaze up.

"Thank you." Vic opened her mouth like she was going to say something else, but then shook her head and looked away.

"What?"

"It's nothing."

"Bullshit. What were you going to say?"

"I was just going to ask if you were working tonight." Vic glanced at her quickly, but it was long enough for Riley to see the hint of attraction in her very expressive blue eyes.

For just a second Riley considered lying, but what good would it do? Vic could end up stopping by the theater to see her again if she thought she was going to be there.

"Actually, I'm off tonight," she said just as the waitress brought their coffees. She watched as Vic added half a sugar packet to hers. "Why?"

"Well, I was hoping maybe you'd consider having dinner with me."

"Are you asking me on a date?" Riley somehow managed not to laugh at the absurdity of it, but then noticed the look of vulnerability on Vic's face. "Wait, really? You're asking me on a date?"

"You're making me second-guess myself here," Vic said with a chuckle as she waved a hand and leaned back. "Forget I asked."

"Hey," Riley said as she reached across the table and covered Vic's hand with her own. When she didn't pull away, Riley met her eyes, wondering where this surge of confidence was coming from. "I would love to have dinner with you."

"You would?" Vic sounded like she didn't believe her.

"Maybe not in this town though?" Riley said with a slight shrug. "A lot of the people we went to school with still live here, and you might be uncomfortable running into them while you're with me."

"I told you last night I don't really care what people think about me," Vic said, turning her hand over to squeeze Riley's gently. "I meant it, Riley. I'd be proud to have people see the two of us together."

"Okay, wow," Riley said, mostly because she wasn't sure what else to say. This couldn't really be happening, could it? Maybe she was having the best dream ever, and if that was the case, she never wanted to wake up. "Have you come out to any of them?"

"I haven't seen any of them since high school ended. None of them ever came out as straight to me, so why should I feel the need to come out to them?" Vic reluctantly let go of Riley's hand when the waitress came with her order. She chuckled at the sheer abundance of food now sitting on the table in front of Riley. "Maybe you won't even be hungry by the time dinner rolls around though."

"I tend to eat a lot when I'm nervous." Riley spread butter over her plate of pancakes before pouring way more syrup over them than Vic had ever seen anyone use.

"Do I make you nervous?" she asked, amused.

"God, yes," Riley said quietly. She hesitated before shoving a forkful of scrambled eggs into her mouth. "Help yourself if you want anything."

Vic just shook her head as she watched her, a smile on her lips. Riley still had the prettiest hazel eyes Vic had ever seen. She allowed herself to get lost in them as Riley continued to eat. After a few moments, she reached over and snagged a slice of bacon. Riley grabbed her wrist with surprising quickness as she shook her head.

"Anything but the bacon," she said with a mischievous glint in her eye.

"Is that so?" Vic held her gaze as she seized the bacon in her other hand and took a bite.

"You'll pay for that, Thayer," Riley said as she let go of her wrist.

"I'll hold you to that, Warren," Vic replied with a wink. She was enjoying this easygoing banter with Riley. She was also enjoying the way the blush creeped up Riley's neck and into her face when she winked at her. Her eyes settled on Riley's mouth and she found herself wondering what it would be like to kiss her. She hoped she'd find out after dinner.

"So, I put in a call to my film distributor," Riley said when she'd finally finished eating. She'd left a couple of bites of pancake on the plate, but everything else was gone. "I can get *Fifty Shades of Grey* for a week from Saturday. That was when you wanted it, right?"

"Oh, my God, that's awesome," Vic said. She made herself sound happier about the news than she really was. Vanessa really did love the movie, but Vic had no desire to sit around with the bitches they'd gone to school with watching a movie many considered to be soft porn. Not exactly her idea of fun. But it wasn't like there was an abundance of venues for a bachelorette party in Wolf Bay. She didn't think a party in the local dive bar would be acceptable to either Vanessa or their mother. "What changed your mind?"

"Honestly? I decided I should give you the benefit of the doubt," Riley said with a shrug. "I really like this side of you, Vic, and I'm sincerely hoping what you're showing me is genuine."

"It is," Vic said, wondering if Riley would ever truly trust her. "I can't tell you how happy this is going to make Vanessa."

"Does she know about it, or is it a surprise?"

"A total surprise." Vic laughed. "She thinks we're just having a dignified dinner and drinks at home with a couple of close friends. She's probably going to kill me, but considering she picked her lesbian sister to be her maid of honor, she should be happy I didn't ask you to book *Showgirls* instead."

"That one I might even get excited about," Riley said with a laugh. "*Fifty Shades* not so much. What time do you want it to start?"

"I was thinking nine thirty, if that works for you. That way we can be sure and be done with dinner and drinks in plenty of time. I can't guarantee none of them will be drunk when they get there, but I'm putting on the invitation that there's no alcohol allowed in the theater."

"I appreciate that," Riley said with a nod. "Although I'm sure someone will sneak a bottle of something in. But, nine thirty it is."

"There will be about twenty or so women there, so if I give you an extra couple hundred, would that cover popcorn and soda for all of them?"

"We can discuss cost later, but I'm sure what you've already offered to pay to rent the theater will cover the cost of concessions as well." Riley looked at her watch. "Wow, it's almost noon already."

"Got a hot date?"

"I certainly hope so," she answered then blushed again. Vic smiled and gave her a nod.

"So do I." She reached for the bill the waitress had left for them some time ago, but Riley swatted her hand away.

"All you had was coffee," she said with a shake of her head. "You aren't paying for my breakfast."

"Fine, but just so there's no confusion later, I'm paying for dinner."

"Deal."

"I'll need your address so I can pick you up."

Riley appeared uncomfortable as her eyes darted around the restaurant. Vic watched in fascination as she suddenly seemed to come to some kind of decision.

"Why don't you pick me up at the theater?"

"Okay," Vic agreed, but wondered why she didn't want her to know where she lived. Maybe she still lived in the trailer park? Not that it would have mattered. "Five o'clock?"

"Perfect," Riley said, looking as if she was finally relaxing. "What should I wear?"

"What you have on would probably be perfectly suitable. It isn't like there are many places around that would qualify as fine dining."

"Then I guess I'll see you later?"

"Yeah." They both stood, and this time the hug they shared wasn't awkward at all. Vic sighed as she let go of her and watched Riley leave the diner. She smiled to herself, amazed she'd actually had the guts to ask Riley on a date. She couldn't believe this was really happening.

Chapter Eleven

R iley looked at her watch for the umpteenth time as she waited for Vic to arrive at the theater. It was still before five, but she'd started preparing herself for what she'd do if Vic didn't show up. When she saw the blue Mercedes pull into a space right in front of the doors, she let out a sigh of relief. She glanced back at Nancy and waved.

"Don't have too much fun," Nancy called out as Riley exited the theater.

Riley was surprised when Vic jumped out of the car and came around to open the door for her. When she saw Vic was wearing slacks and a tailored shirt, she was relieved she'd chosen to wear capri pants and a flowy blouse.

"You look beautiful tonight," Vic said quietly as she walked past and paused before getting into the car.

"And you smell wonderful," Riley replied, taking in the slightly musky scent of Vic's cologne. She had the urge to kiss her, but knew Nancy was probably watching them, so she settled for placing her hand on Vic's forearm for a moment before letting her fingers stray down to her hand. They smiled at each other briefly before Riley got in and Vic hurried back around to the driver's door. "Where are we going?"

"I hope you don't mind, but there's a steakhouse near Hyde Park I want to take you to," Vic said, glancing at her.

"Hyde Park? That's almost an hour away." Riley wondered if the reason was because she liked the restaurant and wanted to take her there, or if she'd decided she really didn't want anyone in Wolf Bay to see them together.

"You do realize you live pretty much in the middle of nowhere, right?" Vic chuckled. "To find a decent restaurant, you'd probably have to go an hour away. I didn't really want to take you to the diner for the second time in one day."

Riley nodded and decided she should just relax and, like Megan urged, see where it goes. She just hoped the place they were going wasn't too expensive. Yes, Vic had said she was going to pay, but Riley wasn't at all sure she was comfortable with that.

They didn't talk much on the drive, and Riley wondered what they were going to find to talk about during dinner. Maybe a date with Vic wasn't the brightest idea she'd ever had. She'd considered more than once telling her to just take her back to Wolf Bay, but despite her misgivings, she wanted to see how the evening played out.

"Wait here," Vic said after she pulled into a parking space and shut the car off. Riley nodded and was curious as to what was happening. She smiled when she realized Vic was merely coming to her side of the car to open the door for her again. She took the hand Vic held out for her and allowed her to help her to her feet. "I hope you're hungry."

"Well, you make me nervous, so..." Riley shrugged as they started for the entrance, but Vic stopped her with a hand to her forearm. She cocked her head to the side and looked at her. "What's wrong?"

"It certainly isn't my intention to make you nervous, so maybe I should do something about it," Vic said as she took a step toward her. Before Riley had a chance to even think about what was happening, Vic framed her face with her hands and leaned in for a kiss. It was chaste, and over before Riley knew it, but her lips tingled just the same. As did other parts of her body if she was being honest. Vic gave her a sexy grin and leaned close to her ear. "Just in case there was any lingering doubt about whether or not this is a date."

"Yeah, that kiss?" Riley pursed her lips and shook her head. "Probably not the best way to calm my nerves."

"No?" Vic looked amused. "Then you'll have to tell me how I can accomplish that. But I'm not sorry I tried it my way first. Are you?"

"Not at all."

"Good. Let's go eat."

❖

God, Vic loved this restaurant. She didn't get to come here nearly enough because it was about a two-hour drive from her penthouse in Manhattan. But they had the best twelve-ounce bone-in ribeye she'd ever tasted. She didn't even open her menu because she knew exactly what she wanted.

"Wow," Riley said, setting her menu down and looking at her from across the table. "This place is a little pricey."

"I told you I was paying, so don't worry about the price," Vic said, waving a hand dismissively. "Seriously. If you want lobster with your steak, order it."

"I've never had lobster."

"Really?" Vic asked, surprised. While she was growing up, they'd had lobster every Sunday night for dinner. One of the perks of being from a family who had more money than they knew what to do with she supposed. "Then you should definitely get it. Everyone needs to try it at least once in their lifetime."

"I just can't see paying this much for a meal, Vic," Riley said, her voice quiet as she glanced around at the other people near them.

"It's worth it, trust me." Vic nodded, but Riley seemed unconvinced. She reached over and took her hand, waiting until

Riley met her eyes. "I asked you on a date, so I'm paying. Please, order whatever you want."

Riley finally nodded with an audible sigh before turning her attention back to the menu. A few minutes later, they gave their orders to the waiter and Vic was pleased when Riley ordered an eight-ounce steak and a lobster tail. She'd been worried she'd try to get nothing but a salad. It was a delightful change of pace though to be having a meal with a woman who didn't seem interested in her money. She just hoped that wouldn't change anytime soon. She used her napkin to wipe a bit of perspiration off her forehead.

"Are you sweating?" Riley asked, the corners of her mouth turning upward.

"Mmm," Vic answered with a nod. "It appears you aren't the only one who's nervous."

"What in the world would you have to be nervous about?"

"I'm here with you," Vic answered, knowing the simple statement was enough of an explanation for her, but Riley stiffened at her words.

"So you are worried someone you know will see us."

"What do I have to do for you to believe I don't care who sees us together?"

"Eat dinner with me closer to home."

"Fine. Next time I will."

"Pretty sure of yourself, aren't you?"

"Not nearly as sure as I let on," Vic said with a small grin. She shrugged at Riley's surprised look. "You scare me, Riley."

"I scare you? Why?"

"I'm afraid you'll never truly see me for the person I am today instead of the person I used to be," Vic said, trying not to let her insecurities stop her from saying the things she truly wanted to say. "I'm worried you might get to know me and decide I'm lacking somehow. That I'm not good enough for you."

"Are you kidding me?" Riley asked, holding her gaze. "Jesus, Vic, if anyone's lacking, it's me. You and I come from two different worlds. I'm afraid your mother will find out about this date and come after me with a shotgun."

"You're forgetting one thing." Vic couldn't stop the grin, even though she knew there was nothing humorous about the situation. "My mother would have to care about me in order to react so strongly. She's made it perfectly clear I am not a part of her family any longer. The only reason Vera's allowing me to stay in her house is because Vanessa chose me to be her maid of honor. Once the wedding is over, things will go back to normal."

"You call your mother Vera?"

"That's what you find odd about what I said?" Vic chuckled, and Riley did as well. "And yes, I do. She visibly cringes if I ever slip and call her Mother."

Once their food came, they stuck to more mundane conversation. Vic waited until they were almost back to Wolf Bay to broach the topic of seeing her again.

"Are you going to the reunion this weekend?"

"Yes," Riley answered, looking at her. "You?"

"I promised Vanessa I'd go," Vic said, rolling her eyes. "But I don't really want to."

"Neither do I, honestly," Riley said. "I promised Megan I'd go."

"Megan? From high school? You're still friends with her?"

"We rent a house together. She's my best friend."

"That's cool," Vic said. She wished she found it easier to make friends. It seemed anyone who worked with her was scared of her, and those who didn't were only interested in what she could do for them. "It's good to have friends. How's your mother?"

"My mother?" Riley turned in her seat, at least as far as the seat belt would allow her to, so she was almost facing her. "I hardly ever see her. In fact, she's in the hospital after suffering from alcohol poisoning, and when she woke up and saw me sitting there, she told me to leave. She didn't want me there. I don't even talk to her unless she calls me looking for money she knows I don't have. What in the world would make you ask about her?"

"Just curious." Vic tried to hide the sadness in her voice. She'd hoped Riley had a better relationship with her mother than she did with her own. She pulled into a parking space by the theater and turned the car off. She undid her seat belt and turned to face Riley. "I had a really nice time tonight."

"So did I, even if dinner did cost half of what I pay for rent every month." Riley looked away from her, but Vic reached out and put a finger under her chin, forcing her to meet her eyes again.

"I enjoyed the company a lot more than the food, so it was worth every penny of what it cost." Vic smiled when Riley did and leaned closer to her. "Can I kiss you good night?"

"Please?" Riley's voice sounded rough, and her eyes were on Vic's lips.

Vic leaned in and placed another chaste kiss on Riley's lips, but Riley made a sound like she disapproved and grabbed her by the collar with both hands, keeping Vic where she was.

"Please tell me that isn't how you kiss a date good night," she said, her breath hot against Vic's mouth. "Because I could tell you why you're single if you do."

Vic didn't need any further encouragement. She let Riley pull her closer until their lips met again, and she immediately ran her tongue along Riley's bottom lip, urging Riley to let her in. When she did, and Vic felt their tongues meet for the first time, she melted into her and moaned quietly.

Kissing Riley was what she assumed kissing an angel would be like. Vic was so lost in the sensations running through her, especially the liquid heat infusing her center. She placed a hand on Riley's hip as Riley's hand moved up her side and her fingers brushed the underside of her breast.

"Jesus, Riley," she said, breathless as their foreheads rested against each other. She looked into her eyes and saw her own arousal mirrored there. "If I'd known you could kiss like that I would have suggested a hotel somewhere in Hyde Park. Unfortunately, I can't invite you back to my place because I share a room with Vanessa. And you share a house with Megan."

"I don't usually fall into bed with someone after the first date," Riley said, regret in her eyes. She traced Vic's face with the fingers of her right hand. "So the hotel would have been a no-go anyway."

"How about the second date?" Vic wiggled her eyebrows, soliciting a deep chuckle from Riley as her thumb moved slowly against the skin on Vic's cheekbone.

"Maybe," she answered with a slight shrug. "How long will you be in town?"

"I go home two weeks from Monday. The day after the wedding." Vic already regretted having to go back to Manhattan. Truth be told she hated it there. She'd much rather be here with Riley, but she had a feeling Riley wouldn't believe her if she were to admit that to her. "Vera wants me out of the house as soon as possible."

"That's too bad," Riley said, looking thoroughly disappointed.

"Can I see you again before the reunion on Saturday? I don't think I can wait six whole days to see you again." Vic sounded needy, but she was beyond caring. She'd had a small taste of Riley, and she had no intention of stopping there.

"I'm off tomorrow." Riley let her hand fall to her lap and leaned back in her seat. "I have to work every other night until Saturday."

"Have dinner with me tomorrow? We'll go wherever you want," Vic said, and Riley nodded quickly. Vic smiled. "Should I pick you up here again? Five o'clock?"

"Yes. Good night, Vic," Riley said before moving in for one more kiss. It was a quick peck on the lips and Vic chuckled at

Riley's groan signaling her frustration at it being chaste. "Play your cards right and there will be more kisses like before in your future."

Vic smiled as she watched Riley get out of the car and head inside the theater. Her entire body was thrumming as if there was a live wire inside her, so she decided to wait a few moments until she got herself under control again.

Because, well, driving distracted was dangerous.

CHAPTER TWELVE

This is really your choice for dinner?" Vic asked once they were seated in the Wolf Bay Diner.

"It is," Riley answered with a nod. She really just needed to see if Vic was going to be all right being seen having dinner with her. In town. Where people who'd known them both in high school would no doubt be. "Are you okay eating here?"

"I'm fine." Vic put her menu down and reached across the table for Riley's hand. "What do I have to do to convince you I don't care who sees us? How about I wait until the place is full, then stand up and declare to everyone that I'm here on a date with Riley Warren?"

"That would be a nice start," Riley said with a sly grin. Vic glanced around the dining area and, seeing there were only a couple of tables empty, she started to stand. Riley gripped her hand tightly and shook her head. "I'm kidding, Vic. You don't have to do it. I just need time to absorb all this. It's not as easy as you might think to get over what I went through in high school. Between my mother treating me like shit at home, and you and your friends harassing me at school, I didn't have much fun during my teen years."

"They were never my friends, Riley," Vic said, looking sincere. Riley tilted her head and stared at her, not really believing it. "They were Vanessa's friends. I'm not proud of it, but yes, I went along with the things they did. For Vanessa, and not for any other reason. I'm not trying to make excuses, okay? I'm owning what I did. By not stopping it, I was complicit in all of it. Our mother was never around when we were younger, so Vanessa and I only had each other. She was my best friend."

Riley was uncomfortable, and she could tell Vic knew it. She tried to pull her hand away, but Vic wouldn't let her. She squeezed it gently until Riley met her eyes across the table. Vic leaned as far over as she could, never breaking eye contact.

"But I am not the same person I was back then. I was scared to death of being bullied by them myself if I tried too hard to distance myself from them. I was a coward. You know the saying better you than me? That was pretty much my motto back then. I'm not proud of it, Riley, and I can't change any of it, no matter how much I want to. All I'm asking is for you to give me the opportunity to show you I've changed."

Riley was spared having to comment on Vic's declarations when their waitress came to get their orders. They hadn't looked over the menu yet, so they asked for a few more minutes. They were silent until after they ordered, and Riley spent most of the time debating with herself whether or not to tell Vic about the darkest day in her life. She figured since Vic had shared what she'd been feeling back then, she might as well too.

"You probably don't remember this, but it's something I've never forgotten," she said before placing her hands in her lap and taking a deep breath. "One day during our senior year, Frank Mills cornered me at my locker, and the rest of his crew was right there with him, including you. He rubbed his crotch against me and basically said he could *make* me like men. I stood up to them, and your sister told me to kill myself."

"I remember it very well." Vic nodded, and she looked as if she might be ill. "I couldn't believe she said it, Riley. God, I wanted to defend you that day, and I did try, however feeble my attempt was. I truly hated every single one of them in that moment. Vanessa included. When I walked away from you, I ran to the bathroom and puked my guts out. I worried all through winter break that you might actually do it."

"I thought about it," Riley said, watching Vic's face closely for an honest reaction. She was a little surprised when she saw what she could only describe as anguish in Vic's eyes. And then there was a couple of tears that ran down her cheeks, and Vic made no move to wipe them away. "Not just because of Vanessa. I don't know what I was thinking by going home and telling my mother about it, but she told me I probably should. She said I would never amount to anything, and no one would ever love me, so I'd probably be better off dead. Let me tell you, hearing that from your own mother is soul-crushing."

"I'm so sorry, Riley," Vic said. She got up and moved to Riley's side of the booth so she could hug her. Riley didn't resist. Being held by Vic felt too good, and she couldn't deny she liked it, probably more than she should. "I wish I'd called you over the break. I'm so happy you made the decision not to do it."

"Megan talked me out of it," Riley said when Vic released her but stayed sitting beside her. "I don't think I really would have done it anyway, but Megan said all the right things to make me feel better about myself."

"Remind me to thank her for that," Vic said with a smile. She tucked a strand of hair behind Riley's ear and let her hand linger on her neck for a moment. As they sat there staring into each other's eyes, Riley felt some of her defenses crumble. This conversation could so easily have made things between them awkward, but Vic had managed to make her feel better about it all. "And can I just say I hate your mother for having said those things to you. No one should be made to feel worthless by their own parents. No one should ever feel death would be the best option, especially a child."

"Hey, we have something in common," Riley said with a chuckle. "We both hate my mother."

"We were friends in grade school," Vic said after a moment. "We weren't besties or anything, but we were friendly. Why did things change?"

"When you're a kid, things like class don't matter as much," Riley said with a shrug. "As we got older, you realized we had no common ground. You had money and I didn't. It was the natural progression of things as I see it."

"Growing up sucks sometimes, doesn't it?" Vic took her hand and held it against her chest. "I sometimes wish we were still kids with none of this baggage between us. Do you think you could ever see me as I am now, and not as I was then?"

"I think you're doing a pretty good job of showing me so far," Riley said quietly. "As much as I still want to hold on to my animosity toward you, you're making it harder to do every time we spend time together."

"Well, I'll take that as a good sign." Vic held Riley's hand to her lips for a moment before releasing her and going back to her own side of the table. "And I'm going to ask you now if you'll go out for a drink with me after the reunion. Maybe we could call it a third date?"

"Maybe," Riley said with a shrug. She couldn't help the grin tugging at the corners of her mouth. "But you'll have to dance with me at least once at the reunion."

"You've got a deal."

"So, why don't you want me to know where you live?" Vic asked as she pulled into a parking space near the movie theater. She turned the engine off and removed her seat belt before turning to see Riley better.

"What?" Riley seemed surprised at the question, but Vic could tell she was stalling. She reached over and took Riley's hand.

"I don't care where you live, you know," she said. "Do you still live in the trailer park?"

"God, no," Riley said, and she visibly shivered. "I think I'd rather be homeless than live in a place like that again."

"Then let me pick you up at your house the next time."

"Pretty sure of yourself, aren't you?"

"What can I say?" Vic grinned. "I'm an optimist."

"Okay, *if* we go out again, you can pick me up at home." Riley leaned closer and placed a kiss on Vic's cheek. "I had a nice time tonight. And I want to thank you for acknowledging the hell you and your friends put me through in high school."

"No problem, I had a nice time too, and it's still early," Vic said as she squeezed her hand. "I mean, it's not even dark out yet."

"Well, unless you want to see a movie, I'm afraid there isn't much else to do in this town."

"I would like to see a movie with you, but not tonight," Vic said. "Maybe we could go for a drive or something."

"Why, Ms. Thayer, are you trying to get me alone somewhere so you can take advantage of me?" Riley smiled and shook her head.

"Maybe," Vic said with a shrug. "Would that be a problem?"

"Honestly? I'm not really sure how to answer that." Riley shook her head but met Vic's eyes. "It's that whole you make me nervous thing, I think."

"Hey, you didn't say no, so I'll take that as a positive."

"You really are an optimist, aren't you?" Riley laughed.

"Being a pessimist is stressful and seems to me to be a waste of energy, so yes," she said with a nod. "I choose to be a positive thinker."

Vic looked at their hands as Riley intertwined their fingers. When she lifted her gaze back to Riley's face, she felt a fluttering in her stomach. Riley was looking at her lips, and Vic knew they were going to kiss. She knew *Riley* was going to initiate it, and it made her inexplicably happy when their eyes met again. Riley reached over and touched her face with her free hand. Vic leaned into it with a small sigh.

"You really are beautiful," Riley said, her voice quiet. She leaned closer and pressed her lips to Vic's. Vic held back, wanting Riley to set the pace. Riley pulled away, causing Vic to let out a small sound of displeasure. "I should go. I'll see you Saturday at the reunion?"

"Yes," Vic said, resigning herself to the fact she would have to wait five whole days to see her again. Riley squeezed her hand briefly before smiling and getting out of the car. Vic watched her as she walked into the theater and wondered what the hell she was doing. She'd never been one to not go after what she wanted. Letting the other woman decide how fast or slow they went was out of character for her.

Somehow though, she knew Riley was different. She felt in her gut if she tried to rush things and push Riley into something, the end result would be Riley running away from her, and she felt that outcome would be devastating for her. And the reason for her letting Riley determine the pace of things was a little scary for her. After her last relationship had gone up in smoke, she decided she wouldn't put her heart on the line ever again. So the realization of what was happening stole her breath away.

Riley is worth it.

Chapter Thirteen

Vic spent the next few days looking at properties she'd set up appointments for before leaving the city. She found one she really liked a few towns over and about twenty minutes from Wolf Bay. She managed to dodge Vanessa's questions about what she was doing going off on her own, but she wished now that she'd mentioned all of this to their father beforehand. If the sale went through, she'd be moving as soon as renovations on the existing house could be completed. She had a feeling he wouldn't be happy if she gave him her two weeks' notice as soon as they arrived back in Manhattan.

Even with that distraction, the few days leading up to when she would be able to see Riley again crawled by for her. She'd wanted nothing more than to go by the theater to visit her, but she didn't want to be seen as a stalker. She managed to keep the empty hours busy helping Vanessa with her wedding preparations and attempting to keep her from going nuts waiting for the big day to arrive. Martin wouldn't be in town until the Friday before the wedding after he was done with work, and Vanessa was going a little stir-crazy.

"Why did you let me talk you into this reunion bullshit?" Vanessa asked as she finished putting on her makeup Saturday after dinner with their parents.

"Excuse me, but it was you who begged *me* to go," Vic told her, looking in the full-length mirror to make sure she looked her best. The suit was a favorite of hers, dark blue and tailored to fit her perfectly. "You know I can't say no to you when you beg."

"I wish you'd learned how to," Vanessa said with a dramatic sigh. She got to her feet and put on her dress before turning her back to Vic and waiting. Vic pulled up the zipper for her and turned her around, her hands on her shoulders.

"So do I, but I haven't quite learned it yet," she said with a wink. "Just think of it as another in a long line of parties you're required to attend for business. Maybe we can get through the night without having to socialize too much with the losers we hung out with in school."

"You know, a couple of those 'losers' are in my wedding party."

"Don't remind me." Vic turned away and went to run a comb through her hair again. Her heart was beating faster, almost as if it knew she'd be seeing Riley soon. She smiled at herself in the mirror.

"Are my scars hidden well enough?" Vanessa asked. "I can change into pants if I have to."

"You look beautiful," Vic said, meeting Vanessa's eyes in the mirror. Her dress went below her knees, and she was wearing boots that covered most of what was exposed of her legs. She turned to face her and smiled. "You can't see anything if you aren't looking for them."

"You're a liar, but thank you. Just don't spend the entire evening canoodling with Riley Warren," Vanessa said. Vic set down the comb and looked at her with a grin.

"Did you really just say *canoodling*?" Vic laughed and shook her head. "Who even says that anymore?"

"Apparently, I do," Vanessa answered before turning on her heel and heading for the stairs. "Come on. Let's get this over with."

She followed Vanessa down the stairs and into the living room where their mother was settled into the couch reading a book. Vera glanced up and then back to the book, but then did a double take upon seeing them.

"For God's sake, Victoria," she said, tossing the book aside. "You're really going to this event dressed like a man?"

"Again, Vera, this is a woman's suit. I am not dressed like a man." Vic ran a hand through her hair as she tried her best not to lash out at her mother. "And I've told you before that I don't like to be called Victoria."

"And I've told you I don't want you in my house, yet here you are." Vera looked pleased with herself. "I guess neither one of us listens to what the other has to say."

"No, we don't, and I wouldn't expect that to change anytime soon."

"We should get going," Vanessa said as she put her arm through Vic's and tried to lead her to the front door.

"You two look like you should be going on a date together," Vera called after them, sounding disgusted.

Vic wisely chose to ignore the comment, but it was obvious Vanessa had had enough. She stopped and turned, stalking back to the living room.

"I am so sick of this bullshit between the two of you," she said, hands on hips. Vic tried not to smile as she watched the look of shock on Vera's face. Vanessa pointed at their mother. "And don't for one second think I blame any of this on her, because it is all on you. So what if she's a lesbian? Daddy doesn't seem to have a problem with it, so why do you? This is the twenty-first century in case you haven't noticed. She's my twin sister and my best friend. She's going to be my maid of honor, and she could wear a metallic rainbow-colored tuxedo to the wedding for all I care."

"How dare you speak to me that way, young lady," Vera said, getting to her feet and taking a few steps toward Vanessa. Vic closed the distance between them and took Vanessa by the elbow, directing her back to the front door. "Don't you turn your back on me!"

"Fuck off, Mother," Vanessa said over her shoulder just before Vic closed the door behind them.

"Holy shit, I can't believe you told Vera to fuck off," she managed to say before doubling over in laughter. "She might change the locks before we get back."

"Good, then I'll uninvite her to my wedding."

"Did you mean what you said?" Vic finally stopped laughing and Vanessa looked at her curiously. "About me wearing a metallic rainbow-colored tuxedo to the wedding?"

"Of course."

"Then I'm calling the tailor first thing Monday morning."

❖

"What's wrong with you tonight?" Megan asked as they headed for the high school gymnasium, the only place in town big enough to hold the reunion. There were no restaurants other than the diner, and a bar seemed too cliché, so the gym it was.

"I'm just a little nervous," Riley admitted. "I haven't seen or heard from her since Monday night. What if it was all just a figment of my imagination?"

"You're such a dork," Megan said, laughing as she playfully shoved her. "Come on, I can't wait to see Peter again. He only comes to town for these things."

Megan grabbed her arm and pulled her toward the main entrance, but Riley quickly scanned the parking lot looking for the blue Mercedes. Her heart dropped when she didn't see it anywhere close to the building. She hadn't been able to stop thinking about Vic since they'd parted. Not even while she was asleep, it seemed. The kiss they'd shared after their first dinner together in Hyde Park had managed to fuel some pretty steamy dreams, and she was hoping she'd get to experience more of the real thing tonight.

But she wasn't naive enough to think Vic would spend a lot of time with her here. Riley was sure she had her own friends to reconnect with. And despite her claims to the contrary, Riley wasn't convinced she didn't really care about what anyone thought of her. The Thayer name meant something in this town, and Riley couldn't imagine Vic purposely sullying their reputation.

Megan squealed—actually *squealed*—when she spotted Peter, the third of their Three Musketeers, which was something only they called themselves back in high school. She released her grip on Riley's arm and ran over to him, throwing her arms around his neck and kissing his cheek. He was laughing when Riley walked up to join them.

"It's so good to see you guys again." Peter let go of Megan and hugged Riley. "You know you two are the only reason I ever come back to this godforsaken town, right? I can't believe neither of you have ever left."

Even Riley could admit he'd grown into a handsome man. He'd been the typical geek back in school—thick glasses, *Star Wars* T-shirts, and video games had been his signature things. Now he was physically fit, wore contacts, and cleaned up nicely. In fact, he looked more like he belonged with the cool kids than with them. Although, looking around, Riley noticed a lot of the so-called "cool kids" were now overweight and balding. And the women wore way too much makeup in their attempts to look as if they were still eighteen.

"You guys want anything to drink?" Riley asked, feeling like she was a third wheel. Funny, she'd never felt that way before, but Megan was looking at Peter as though she might devour him right there in front of everyone. To be fair, he had the same look in his eye when he was looking at her.

"No, thanks," they both said and started laughing. Riley rolled her eyes and made her way toward the cash bar in the corner, which was so odd to her. Really? A cash bar in a high school gymnasium? Only in Wolf Bay.

"Hey, Warren, you ready to give up the ladies and see what you've been missing?"

Riley stopped and turned to face Frank Mills. He'd been the captain of the football team, and one of her main tormentors, but he was now a good fifty pounds heavier and was sporting a ridiculous looking comb-over. He'd never shown up for a reunion before, and she'd wrongly assumed she'd never see him again.

"Not really, but if you are, I know a nice man I could set you up with." She walked away before he could stop sputtering and think of a response, and she just chuckled. What an asshole.

She ordered a beer and turned to make her way back to Megan but was met by Frank and a few of his closest friends. She sighed, knowing what was probably coming. She didn't care. She was so over it all. She'd made it through high school, and she'd make it through this evening no matter what they threw her way.

"You can't say something like that and then just walk away, you fucking dyke." Frank sneered at her, as if that was going to scare her. She was in better shape than he was and had no doubt she could take him one-on-one.

"Are we really doing this?" Riley asked, looking from one person to another. She was relieved to see that at least a few of them looked uncomfortable with the situation. Maybe Frank was the only one who hadn't grown up over the past twenty years. She held his gaze as she spoke. "You don't scare me, Frank. I'll admit you did back in the day, but now? You're nothing but a poor excuse for a man. I feel sorry for your wife."

A couple of the people hooted at that, and Riley smirked as she walked away, leaving him sputtering once again. It felt good to stand up to him for once. The rest of his crew pretty much left her alone at the previous reunions, and some of them were customers at the theater and had even been nice to her. They weren't her friends by any stretch of the imagination, but they all seemed to have changed. Except Frank.

Her attention was drawn toward the entrance of the gym and her step faltered when she saw Vic and Vanessa walking in. There was absolutely no mistaking they were identical twins, but they looked so very different. Vanessa was wearing a rather expensive looking dress with some sexy ass boots and was wearing makeup. Vic, on the other hand, was wearing a suit that fit her like a glove and her hair was slicked back. Their eyes met across the gym, and Vic smiled at her before leaning close to Vanessa and saying something that caused her to look in her direction too. She felt a little light-headed when they both started walking toward her.

"Riley, it's so nice to see you when my face isn't covered in blood and my legs aren't on fire," Vanessa said as she held Riley's hand between both of hers. Riley was taken aback by the self-deprecating humor coming out of the woman who used to torment her. She glanced at Vic, who simply shrugged. "I'm sorry, that was probably too much, wasn't it? But really, I want to thank you for what you did. I was told I probably wouldn't have survived if not for you."

"Anyone would have done the same," she said, shifting her weight from one foot to the other. She hadn't gotten much in the way of gratitude, or any kind of praise for that matter, growing up, so she was a little uncomfortable with it now. "But you're welcome."

"I'm going to assume you two don't need a chaperone and I'm going to see if I can find anyone I wouldn't mind hanging out with for a bit," Vanessa said before whispering something in Vic's ear that made her nod and roll her eyes.

"It was nice to see you again, Riley," Vanessa said. "And I really want to offer an apology for the way we treated you back in high school. I truly am sorry."

"Thanks," Riley said, but it came out sounding more like a question. She looked at Vic who once again simply shrugged.

"That's Vanessa for you," she said. "She never sits still for long in any social situation."

"What did she say that caused you to roll your eyes?"

"Oh, you saw that, did you?" Vic laughed as she placed her hand on the small of Riley's back. "She told me to not spend all evening in a corner somewhere with you."

"You don't have to hang out with me, you know," Riley said, stiffening slightly at the words.

"But I want to," Vic said, looking at her strangely. "Surely after our two dates you realize that."

"Well, I hadn't heard from you since, so I wasn't sure." God, Riley hated feeling so insecure. She glanced around to see if anyone was watching them. Her eyes met Frank Mills's and she looked away quickly. "Maybe you shouldn't touch me."

"I'm sorry?" Vic was obviously perplexed.

"People are watching."

Vic looked around the room and seemed to stop momentarily when she saw Frank watching them. Riley followed her line of vision until her gaze settled on Vanessa who was talking with someone Riley didn't recognize.

"You mean Frank Mills?" Vic said as she met her eyes. Riley nodded and Vic laughed. "Let him look. He's just jealous because he doesn't have a date as beautiful as I do. He's an asshole, and he always has been. I seriously don't know what Vanessa ever saw in him."

"It really doesn't bother you?"

"Riley, I'd kiss you right here in front of everyone. If they can't tell by the way I look that I'm a lesbian, then they probably wouldn't even understand what I was saying if I came right out and said it to them." Vic looked down and grasped her hand before leading her over to some tables that had been set up along the walls of the gym. "It really doesn't bother me. The only thing that matters to me is if maybe you don't feel comfortable being seen with me?"

"No, of course not." Riley smiled at her as she shook her head. They were sitting next to each other and Vic's hand was resting on Riley's thigh. Riley covered it with her own and sighed contentedly.

"Good." Vic nodded once and brought Riley's hand to her lips for a brief kiss. She smiled so big it made Riley's heart swell.

"I can't believe we're sitting here in the gym twenty years after we left this place, holding hands. And under that banner too."

Vic pointed above them to the banner that sported the words *Hopes and Dreams,* the theme of their senior prom. They both laughed and rolled their eyes.

"It was corny as hell back then, but now it makes a little more sense, right?" Riley asked. "I mean, I didn't go to prom, so I guess it was just corny in my mind."

"You want to know a secret?" Vic said, leaning close to Riley. "I didn't go to prom either, and you're right, it was corny."

"What? How did I never know you skipped prom? Isn't that something everyone would have been talking about?"

"Everyone was so caught up in their own meaningless shit, I guess it didn't matter who did or didn't show up."

"What were your hopes and dreams back then?" Riley asked, glancing back at the banner.

"Oh, my God," Vic said before leaning forward and resting her elbows on the table. She turned her head to look at Riley, wondering how much to reveal. She didn't even know what to dream when she was a teenager. "All I really cared about was not feeling as confused as I was for the rest of my life. And I wanted to be comfortable in my own skin, because I definitely was not back then. What about you?"

Riley shook her head and looked away, making Vic wonder what she didn't want to say. She didn't push, sensing Riley would answer when she was ready. A shadow fell over the table and Vic glanced up at Frank.

"Hey, Victoria," he said, sounding overly cheerful.

"It's Vic," she told him, trying to ignore the way her stomach turned. He gave her the creeps. He always had.

"What?" he asked, looking truly perplexed.

"I want to be called Vic now."

"Whatever," he mumbled as he glanced over his shoulder at the few couples who were dancing. "Come dance with me."

"I'm sorry, was that a question?" Vic saw Riley looking at her in her peripheral vision but never looked away from Frank.

"Come on, you know you always wanted a piece of this," he said with a grin that threatened to turn her stomach. At least he didn't grab his crotch like he had in high school every time he said something suggestive.

"Yeah, maybe to put through a wood chipper." Vic laughed because Riley did, and her stomach turned for an entirely different reason at the sound of it.

"What the fuck is that supposed to mean?" He looked between Vic and Riley, but they just kept laughing.

"Maybe you should go find one of your buddies to explain it to you," Vic said.

"Hey, Frank, you know earlier when you asked if I was ready to give up the ladies?" Riley asked. Vic looked at her, then up to Frank, trying to resist the urge to slug him for still trying to bully Riley.

"Yeah, what about it?"

"Would you give this up," Riley placed her hand on Vic's shoulder and glanced at her with a smile. "If *you* had it?"

"Yeah, right," he said with a loud snort. "Like I'd ever believe Victoria Thayer is a dyke."

Riley looked at her again and quirked one eyebrow in question. Not knowing what to expect, Vic just nodded. She had a feeling whatever Riley had planned would put Frank in his place, and she was all for it. Riley stood and faced Vic, who moved her chair back a bit from the table.

"If you don't want me to do this, tell me," Riley said, her voice low enough so only Vic could hear her.

"I don't know what's going on in your head, but I'm game no matter what it is," Vic replied with a smile. She was a little surprised when Riley straddled her and slid her arms around her neck, but not so much that she didn't fall right into it and placed her hands firmly on Riley's hips. "I could really get used to this."

Vic closed her eyes as Riley leaned in, pressing their lips together. Vic wasn't sure how much of a show Riley intended to put on, so she decided to let her have total control. She moaned into her mouth when Riley's tongue slid between her lips. Vic moved her hands up Riley's sides and loved the way she pressed down against her lap in response.

"Jesus, you're both sick in the head," Frank said amidst the whistles and applause in the background.

"God, can you kiss," Riley said, breathless as she pulled back slightly and looked her in the eye. She started to get off her, but Vic held her in place.

"You do amazing things to me, Riley Warren." Vic enjoyed the feeling of wonderment that overtook her. "No one has ever been able to turn me on so thoroughly, so fast. What do you say we get out of here and go somewhere a little more private?"

"Mother," she said, placing a hand on Vic's chest before moving it to her own. "And roommate, remember?"

"There's got to be a hotel somewhere fairly close, right?" Vic was close to begging, and she didn't even care. She wanted Riley so bad she could almost taste it.

Riley let her head fall back and she laughed before getting up and moving back to her own chair. Vic looked up and saw Frank still standing rooted to his spot, staring at them.

"We're both sick in the head, but you seem fine with watching us," Vic said, trying hard not to appear as frustrated as she felt. "Go to hell, Frank."

"Fucking dykes," he said as he turned and walked away.

"I think I just outed you to our entire graduating class," Riley said with a smirk.

"Good. It saves me from having to sit down and have any conversations with these idiots."

"They aren't all bad," Riley said with a shrug. "But he most definitely is King Idiot."

"So," Vic said, turning in her seat to face Riley. "Your hopes and dreams?"

"You don't give up, do you?"

"Not very easily."

"Fine." Riley looked away again, and Vic thought she was going to avoid answering, but then she turned to face her again as she sighed. "All I wanted was to survive high school, and to not allow my mother to suck me into the rabbit hole she'd decided to go down."

"And now?" Vic asked, not knowing how to respond to what she'd said. They all knew Riley's mother was an alcoholic, and after their previous conversation Riley knew how Vic felt about her, but she wasn't going to say anything else derogatory about her. "Tell me what you want now."

"I want to own the movie theater I work at." Riley didn't look at her as she spoke the words, so she didn't see Vic's reaction to them.

Her heart sped up, and she wondered if she'd read Riley wrong. Maybe she was simply after her money. Of course, she hadn't asked Vic for money, but this was how it always started. A suggestion here and there. She glanced around the room and saw Vanessa watching them.

"So, you want to spend the rest of your life here in Wolf Bay?" Vic asked her after her moment of panic receded.

"I don't really know anything else," Riley said with a shrug. "I'm happy here for the most part, so I haven't ever considered moving away. What about your hopes and dreams now?"

"I want to find a woman to share the rest of my life with who cares more about me than she does my money and what it can do for her." Riley must have heard the edge to her voice because she tilted her head and looked confused.

"Wait, you don't think I was asking you for money, do you?" Riley shook her head and looked offended at the prospect. "I couldn't care less about your money, Vic. If I'm ever going to buy the theater, I'm going to do it on my own."

"I'm sorry," Vic said, feeling like a jerk for jumping to conclusions. "You have to understand though that I'm used to women dating me because of what I can do for them. I would give up all my money to live a simpler and happier life."

"Says the woman who's never had to live without money," Riley said with a chuckle. "Living paycheck to paycheck isn't all it's cracked up to be, you know."

"You know, it's true what they say," Vic said, watching Riley's face. "Money can't buy happiness. Trust me, I've tried."

Vic really didn't want to talk about this anymore. She absolutely hated talking about money. Honestly, she had so much of it she didn't even need to work another day in her life. Her grandparents had seen to that, much to her mother's dismay.

Vera had been convinced her in-laws shared her views on Vic's lesbianism and wouldn't leave her a thing when they died. Not only did they support Vic in everything she did, they'd left her even more money than anyone expected because they'd worried Vera would cut her off eventually. Thanks to some smart investments, she'd built up quite the little nest egg for herself.

"Seriously, do you want to get out of here?" Vic asked when Riley remained silent. "You're the only one I care about spending time with, and we could go for a drive or something. No pressure."

"Sure," Riley said with a nod.

Vic went to tell Vanessa she was leaving, and Riley went to tell Megan. They met each other just outside the entrance and made their way to Riley's vehicle. It was only eight o'clock so it was still light out, and Riley suggested a drive to the next town where they could get a couple of awesome ice cream cones. Riley and ice cream. Vic couldn't think of a better way to spend an evening.

CHAPTER FOURTEEN

"Too bad there isn't a drive-in around," Vic said as they sat in the back of Riley's SUV with their feet hanging over the edge, eating their ice cream.

"Really?" Riley asked without looking at her. She appeared too intent on not letting her ice cream melt. "I show movies for a living, and you want me to spend my night off watching one?"

"Oh, I can pretty much guarantee there wouldn't be any movie watching going on." Vic bumped her lightly with her shoulder and laughed when Riley looked at her incredulously.

"And just what are you suggesting?"

"I'm suggesting that if you don't stop licking your ice cream like that, I might just have to rip your clothes off and take you right here in front of all these families."

"Like what?"

"Like I can picture it being me you're using your tongue on."

"Fuck," Riley said under her breath as she squirmed a little.

"Yes, that's exactly what I'm suggesting." Vic bumped her again, but Riley refused to look at her this time.

"Who knew ice cream was foreplay for you?" Riley asked with a chuckle.

"All you had to do was ask."

"There's nowhere to do it, and I am not doing it in the car, so you can just get that thought out of your head right now." Riley finished her cone and wiped her fingers on the napkin she'd grabbed at the counter.

"If you don't want to have sex with me, just say so."

"I do want to, Vic, and I think you know it." Riley got up and walked to the trash can to get rid of her napkin and took her time walking back. She met Vic's eyes and held them as she placed her hands on either side of her hips and leaned closer. "I just know you're leaving after the wedding, and who knows if we'll ever see each other again? I don't do well with casual hookups, okay?"

"Knowing you're here, and that you'd want to see me again, I wouldn't stay away for long," Vic told her, hoping she believed her. She'd never said anything more true to a woman. "You are an amazing woman, and I know casual would never be enough with you."

"You are a charmer, aren't you?" Riley grinned and stood up straight, her arms crossed over her chest. She shook her head and glanced down at her feet. "But even if you mean that—*especially* if you mean it—then I think we should take things a little slow. Don't take this the wrong way, but up until a few days ago, I'd only known you as Victoria Thayer, the bitch from high school. I think I'd like to get to know you a little better before jumping into a physical relationship."

"I can respect that," Vic said with a nod, even though she wanted nothing more than to jump into bed with her in that moment. "I don't have to like it, but I can respect it."

"Good. Then come on, I want to show you something."

❖

Riley was disappointed they didn't make it back to her house before the sunset, but she took Vic out onto the rooftop where there were Adirondack chairs and a small table between them. She brought her Bluetooth speaker out also and turned on some music to listen to while they sat and enjoyed the evening.

"This is amazing." Vic gazed at the stars overhead as though she'd never seen them before. "I'd forgotten how many stars you can see here. You can't see any in the city."

"It would have been even more amazing if we'd made it in time to see the sun go down behind the Catskills." Riley was up here every night she wasn't working just to watch the sunset.

"I can imagine." Vic held her hand out on the table between them, and Riley took it, entwining their fingers together. "When's your next night off?"

"Monday," she said quietly, looking at their hands as Vic smoothed her thumb over the back of hers. "I would have been off tomorrow, but I had to switch with one of my assistant managers in order to have tonight off for the reunion."

"Maybe we could make a date to meet here for the sunset?"

"I'd like that. I could cook dinner for you. What do you like to eat?"

"I'm not picky."

"Meat loaf?" Riley asked, expecting her to balk at the suggestion.

"I would love meat loaf." Vic chuckled, obviously suspecting Riley thought she would say no. "When's the next day off after that?"

"Not until next Sunday," Riley said. Even though she loved her job, she hated the hours. She had to be there pretty much all the time, but Sunday through Wednesday were the best days, business-wise, to take off. And if her assistants needed time off, she ended up sacrificing her two days off, like this week. But sitting here looking at Vic, she didn't regret it one bit.

"Then I would like to ask you on another date for next Sunday." Vic was looking at her expectantly, but Riley didn't say anything right away.

"Are you trying to monopolize all my time off?" she finally asked, still staring up at the sky.

"God, yes," Vic said with a chuckle. "I'm only here for two more weeks, and I want to spend as much time as I can with you. And I would like to ask you on a date for the following Sunday as well."

Riley looked at her, and Vic could swear she saw confusion at first, but then the reason she would ask for a date on that particular day seemed to click in Riley's mind. She shook her head vehemently.

"No, I am not going to Vanessa's wedding with you." God, she hated weddings. She hated getting dressed up, and she despised all the love in the air. It made her think too much about what she didn't have.

"Not the wedding, the reception," Vic said, squeezing her hand. She tried to turn in her seat, but the chair wasn't cooperating. "Damn it, I love the way these chairs look, and they're comfortable, but they can succeed in making the most coordinated person look like a complete fool when you try to stand up."

Riley giggled, mostly because she agreed with her. "Then don't stand up and I won't laugh at you."

Vic narrowed her eyes but couldn't stop grinning. "I would never ask you to attend a wedding my mother has spent way too much time and money planning. The ceremony will no doubt be a display of my family's wealth. But will you please be my date for the reception?"

"Won't you be sitting next to your sister since you're the maid of honor?"

"Usually, yes, that's where I would be expected to sit. But I seriously hate being the center of attention, and since my mother hates *me*, we've come to the agreement that I will be sitting at the first table instead of being up with the rest of the family and the wedding party."

"I'm sure she doesn't hate you," Riley said, and she was surprised when Vic snorted laughter. "That was an interesting sound."

"I'm going to glide right over that unfortunate incident and hope it never happens again." Vic's cheeks reddened, and Riley thought she'd never seen anything more adorable, although she thought it best to not say it out loud. "Trust me when I say she absolutely does, and I'm okay with it because the feeling is completely mutual. I have my father, and my sister, and they're all I need. But I'm not letting you change the subject. Will you go with me?"

"You just don't want to have to fight off all the single men who ask you to dance."

"I'll admit while that is an appealing perk, it is not the reason I want you to go, believe me." Vic looked up at the stars again and sighed. "I enjoy spending time with you, and I'm not looking forward to having to return to the city the following day. I really do want to spend all the time I possibly can with you before I leave. I want to know everything there is to know about you, Riley Warren."

Riley wasn't quite sure how to respond. It was so easy to forget Vic's time in town had an expiration date, and she really didn't like thinking about it. And honestly, there wasn't all that much to know. Riley was an open book. She had no father, her mother was an alcoholic who neglected her growing up, and she worked far too much. How interesting would her life possibly be to a woman like Vic?

"I had a crush on you in high school," she said, and immediately wished she hadn't spoken those words. God, how embarrassing. She pulled her hand away and stood to walk over to the edge of the roof.

"God damn chair," she heard Vic mutter and turned to see her looking decidedly ungraceful as she tried to get to her feet. She met Riley's eyes and pleaded with her. "A little help?"

Riley walked back to her and held her hand out, which Vic took without a word, and pulled her out of the chair. She let go immediately and went back to the edge, but Vic was right there with her, putting her arms around her middle and pulling her so Riley's back was flush against Vic's front. She rested her chin on Riley's shoulder and spoke directly into her ear, causing goose bumps all over her body.

"Tell me about your crush," she said.

"I shouldn't have said anything."

"But you did, so now I want to know," Vic said before placing a light kiss right below her ear. "Why didn't you ever tell me?"

"Seriously? You were a part of the cool kid clique who bullied me relentlessly," Riley said. She wanted to pull out of her embrace, but it felt too good. "Why the hell would I say anything and risk even more of it?"

"I'm sorry, you're absolutely right," Vic said, tightening her hold on her and nuzzling her neck. "I probably wouldn't have been receptive to it back then but, looking back, I'm pretty sure I had a crush on you too."

"You're so full of shit."

"No, I'm being serious here." Vic sighed, and the exhale of breath tickled her ear. "I didn't know for sure until college that I was a lesbian, but you…you confused the hell out of me. I was nothing more than a big bundle of nerves around you. In fact, I was so anxious around you I became physically sick sometimes."

"I just thought you hated me." Riley turned in her arms and looked her in the eye.

"I think that's what I wanted you to think," Vic said with a crooked smile. "I think in my underdeveloped teenaged mind, I was under the impression that if you hated me, I wouldn't feel those things anymore."

"Yeah?" Riley asked as she tilted her head to the side. "How'd that work out for you?"

"It didn't. You hated me all right, but it just amplified the confusion and nervousness."

Riley stared into her eyes, looking for any kind of sign to indicate she was lying, but there was nothing other than sincerity looking back at her. She placed a hand on Vic's cheek and her stomach fluttered when Vic leaned into the touch. She felt her pulse kick up a notch or two before she moved closer and pressed her lips against Vic's. Their kiss started out slow and sexy, but soon turned into something more akin to desperation. Vic's hands moved down to Riley's ass and pulled her body even tighter against hers, causing Riley to groan.

"Fuck," Vic said as she put a little distance between them. "I should go."

"No," Riley said, surprising even herself. "Stay."

"I thought you wanted to take things slow," Vic said, her pupils dilating and telegraphing her arousal to Riley.

"I did. I do," she said. "Do you think we could sleep in the same bed and not have sex?"

"If that's what you want," Vic said with a slow nod. "I would do anything for you, Riley."

"If you can keep your hands to yourself, then I will go with you to the wedding reception."

"Does that mean I can't hold you?"

"You can hold me. You can even kiss me," Riley said as she took her by the hand and led her back to the stairs that would lead them to her bedroom. "Just don't try and get in my pants."

CHAPTER FIFTEEN

Vic woke with a start, slightly disoriented because she wasn't immediately sure of where she was. But then she realized she had a warm body pressed against her front and looked down to see Riley sound asleep. She smiled and held her a little tighter.

She'd been surprised the night before when Riley had confessed she had a crush on her twenty years ago. This was all so surreal. She closed her eyes and took in the scent of Riley's slightly coconut shampoo. If this was a dream, she didn't want to wake up.

This wasn't like her, she had to admit. She didn't share a bed with a woman she hadn't had sex with, but this felt so right. *Riley* felt so right. She stiffened slightly when Riley shifted, but then she stilled again with a soft sigh. Vic relaxed, but she wanted nothing more than to make love to Riley. She looked down again and saw they were both dressed, just not in the clothes they'd worn to the reunion. Vic remembered Riley giving her a pair of shorts and a T-shirt to sleep in, and Riley was dressed the same.

She should probably leave. Vanessa was no doubt worried about her, but she abhorred the thought of getting out of this bed. She started to pull her arm away from Riley where it was snug against her stomach, but Riley's hand gripped her wrist and pulled it closer to her, resting it between her breasts.

"Jesus, Riley, you're killing me," she whispered. Riley burrowed back into her, moving her ass against Vic's crotch. She sucked in a breath, not wanting to wake her. She stayed still for a few minutes, just listening to Riley breathe, but then couldn't deny any longer that she had to pee. Badly. She somehow managed to slip out of the bed without waking her up and grabbed the clothes she'd worn the previous night before disappearing into the bathroom attached to Riley's bedroom.

After she was dressed, she used a bit of Riley's toothpaste and brushed her teeth with her finger before exiting the bathroom and stopping for a moment to look at her. She'd curled herself around the pillow Vic had used and was holding it tightly. Vic wanted to wake her up but knew it would be a bad idea. Mostly because she had no doubt she wouldn't want to leave if she did.

She started for the kitchen but stopped when she heard the front door open. Probably Megan coming in from getting the morning paper. Megan jumped and put a hand over her heart when she saw Vic standing there.

"Holy shit," she said. "You scared the hell out of me."

"Sorry," Vic said, but she was smiling as she took note of the fact she wasn't the only one wearing last night's clothes. "Just coming home?"

Megan blinked at her for a moment before removing her shoes and walking into the kitchen, Vic following a few steps behind. "I'm not even sure how you could think that's any of your business."

"You're right, I'm sorry again," Vic said, leaning against the counter and crossing her arms over her chest. Megan had begun making coffee but stopped and turned to look her up and down.

"I see *you* haven't made it home yet."

Vic fought the urge to squirm under her scrutiny. She was sorry to say she wouldn't even have recognized Megan if she hadn't known she was Riley's roommate. And given the way Megan was eyeing her, she wondered if she was in the same boat.

"No, I haven't."

"You know, I never could tell the two of you apart, but I'm going to make an educated guess and say you're Victoria."

"Vic, please," she said with a nod. "Good guess, considering Vanessa is marrying a man in two weeks. Wouldn't that be quite the scandal. Not sure my mother's heart could take a shock that big."

Megan chuckled and resumed getting the coffee ready. "Are you staying for breakfast?"

"Riley is still asleep, so probably not." Vic unconsciously glanced up the stairs toward Riley's bedroom. When she refocused on Megan, she saw she was being watched again.

"She's my best friend." Megan wiped her hands on a dish towel as she spoke. "If you hurt her, I swear to God I will hunt you down and kill you myself."

"Down, girl," Vic said, putting her hands up in front of her and shaking her head. "I find it admirable, and honestly would expect no less, but I have no intention of hurting her. In fact, I have the feeling I may be the one who ends up hurt."

"How do you figure?"

"I care a great deal for Riley," Vic said, looking down at her feet. She really should be telling Riley this, and not her best friend. But she knew she needed to convince Megan if she had any hope of ever convincing Riley. "But I strongly suspect once I go back to the city, I may never see her again unless I'm the one who comes back here. Am I right?"

"Probably. Riley's never been one to travel too far from home. She'd never admit it, but I think she worries too much about her mother. Personally, I think she should cut off all ties to the woman, but she won't listen to me." Megan sighed and glanced at the ceiling. "It's not as if she ever really acted like a mother, you know?"

"No, I don't," Vic said, wondering at the knowledge they had both grown up with mothers who weren't really mothers. Maybe it was an epidemic in Wolf Bay. "Are you close with your mother?"

"What does that have to do with anything?"

"Nothing." Vic put her hands up again and decided it was time to get out of there. She really didn't mean to continually put Megan on the defensive. "I should go."

"Wait, you said she was still asleep," Megan said, shaking her head in obvious confusion. "You're just going to leave without saying anything to her? Do you make a habit of sleeping with women and running out before they wake up?"

"Whoa, I think we have a misunderstanding here." Vic chuckled, which seemed to make Megan even angrier if the red tinge to her cheeks was any indication. "We didn't sleep together. Well, we did *sleep* together, but we didn't have sex. Not that I don't want to, but Riley wants to take things slow. And really, it isn't any of your business what I make a habit of doing, because Riley means so much more to me than any...you know what? I'm babbling. Tell Riley I'll call her later, okay? It was nice to see you again, Megan."

She turned and walked out the front door before realizing she'd ridden there with Riley the night before. She pulled out her phone and called Vanessa when she got a few houses away.

"Where the hell are you?" Vanessa asked as she answered the call.

"Good morning to you too," she replied with a sigh. "I need you to come pick me up."

"Mother is furious, you know." Vic didn't miss the tinge of happiness in Vanessa's voice at the declaration. "She's actually wandering around the house muttering to herself about how she never should have let you stay here."

"Good," Vic said. She walked around the corner and found herself standing in front of the diner. She told Vanessa where she was. "I'm glad I could be the cause of her inevitable nervous breakdown."

"I'll be there in twenty minutes. And don't think I'm at all happy about you forcing me to drive."

❖

"Tell me everything," Vanessa said the second Vic got into the car. "I have to live vicariously through you now, you know."

"There's nothing to tell." Vic closed her eyes and leaned her head against the headrest.

"Bullshit," Vanessa said, slowly pulling out onto the road and heading toward the house. "Everybody saw the lap dance she gave you last night, and you left with her right after. You can't convince me you didn't have sex with her."

"It wasn't a lap dance. Frank was giving us a hard time, and he didn't believe I was a lesbian. She decided to prove it to him."

"Jesus, Vic, if you're doing this to get under Vera's skin, I'd say mission accomplished."

"What the hell does that mean?" Vic looked at her, surprised.

"You've made your point. You can stop cozying up to the trailer trash."

"What the fuck, Vanessa?"

"Come on, are you trying to tell me you actually like her?" Vanessa glanced at her with an incredulous look on her face, and Vic had to tamp down the urge to slug her. "I mean, come on, she was such an easy target. Secondhand clothes, some of which were donated to charity by our own mother, an alcoholic mother and no father. You can't be serious."

"Let me out." Vic was amazed her voice sounded so calm, because she was anything but.

"Don't be stupid."

"Are you forgetting she actually saved your life, Vanessa?"

"I thanked her, and now I can move on."

"Stop the fucking car and let me out. Now."

Vanessa slammed on the brakes and turned to look at her. Vic just shook her head and stared out the windshield for a moment before reaching for the door handle. Vanessa's hand on her arm made her pause for a moment.

"Vic, I'm sorry, okay? You know I want you to be happy, but do you honestly think you can be happy with her? Think about what you're doing. Think about what your last name is, for God's sake."

Vic yanked her arm away from her and got out of the car. Before closing the door, she leaned down and looked back in at her.

"You're no different than her. God, how could I never have seen it? And for your information, I don't give a damn about our last name. It's meant nothing but pain and suffering for me most of my life. You can fuck off."

She slammed the door and walked to the edge of the road, wondering which way to go. Vanessa pulled the car over and got out, looking serious as she walked toward her.

"Have I got you good and riled up?"

"What?" Vic was thoroughly confused.

"Frank was at the house this morning talking to Vera." Vanessa stood a couple of feet away from her, her hands firmly on her hips. "I don't know what they were saying, but I can sure as hell guess. I thought I'd get you all worked up so you wouldn't be blindsided by her when we got home."

"Wait, so…this was all an act?"

"Of course it was. You know me better than that, Vic. You know I always have your back." Vanessa shook her head and looked away for a moment. "I'll admit I don't really know what you see in her, and I think she's just going to break your heart like every other woman has because she only wants your money, but what the hell? You're only in town for another two weeks right? Then you'll probably never see her again. Have fun while you can."

"She's different," Vic said with a quiet conviction.

"If you say so," Vanessa said with a shrug. "Now get back in the car. Save your anger for Vera when we get home. And you're driving."

Chapter Sixteen

V ic was still pissed at Vanessa when they walked into the house a few minutes later. They hadn't spoken to each other the rest of the ride, and Vic was barely keeping her anger at bay. She wanted to believe it was only to prepare her for Vera's coming tirade, but she also knew Vanessa had really hated Riley back in high school. For no good reason, really. So when they ran into their mother at the bottom of the steps and Vera gave her a look of undisguised contempt, she started to lose the tenuous hold on her emotions.

"You look like you have something to say, Vera," she said, stopping only a few inches away from her. "So why don't you just go ahead and say it?"

Vera took a moment to look at her, and then Vanessa before settling back on Vic. "What the hell do you think you're doing with that piece of trash?"

"If I were you, I'd be really careful how I spoke about Riley."

"Are you threatening me?" Vera stood taller and tried to look menacing, but Vic laughed. She couldn't help it. Then Vera's face turned a nice shade of red which only caused Vic to laugh more. "I'm still your mother, and you will not speak to me that way."

"Oh, really? So when you told me back in college, when I came out to you and Dad, that I was no longer your child you didn't actually mean it? Is that what you're saying? Because I was pretty sure you meant it, and so was Dad. Which is why he never pushed me to come back here all these years. He knew you didn't want me around."

"You're trying to change the subject."

"No, you did that." Vic was breathing hard with the effort to not let this altercation get out of hand. "But let me bring us back around to the subject at hand. What I'm doing is spending time with a woman I genuinely like and care for. And nothing you can say or do will make me stop seeing her."

Vic looked at Vanessa, who was still standing right beside her but wisely keeping out of it. There was no doubt she could see how thoroughly incensed she was. She gave Vanessa a small smile as she remembered what she'd asked Riley the night before and turned back to Vera.

"I've asked her to come to the wedding reception with me."

"That woman will not set foot in this house, do you understand me?" Vera asked, looking for all the world as though she was going to lash out at her.

"Then move the reception," Vic said quietly. "Because she is going to be my date."

"What the hell is going on in here?" their father asked as he emerged from the living room. He looked between the three of them as he folded his paper under his arm. "I'll accept an explanation from any of you, by the way."

Vic folded her arms over her chest but never looked away from her mother. She knew Vera would put on a show for him like she always did, so she decided to wait it out.

"She's bringing that—"

"Careful, Vera," Vic warned her.

"She's bringing Riley Warren," Vera began. Vic smiled at the way her mother had to force the name past her lips, "to Vanessa's wedding reception."

"That's wonderful!" He walked over to Vic and embraced her tightly as he spoke into her ear. "Don't worry about your mother. I'll deal with her."

"What is wrong with you?" Vera nearly shouted. "That girl is nothing but trash."

"I can't wait to meet her," he said to Vic before turning back to their mother. "Vera, I want a word with you. Upstairs. *Now.*"

Vic and Vanessa watched in stunned silence as their mother turned and stomped up the stairs, their father right behind her. Vic couldn't remember a time when he'd ever stood up to her. As far as she knew, he was as afraid of her as they were.

"Well, that was fun," Vanessa said, grabbing Vic's hand.

"Really? This is your idea of fun? There's a reason I don't come home for holidays, and it has everything to do with that woman." She squeezed Vanessa's hand quickly and let go. "You're okay with me bringing her?"

"You can bring whoever you want. Just promise me you'll dance with her."

"Why do I get the feeling you only want her there to make Vera's day a miserable one?"

Riley was disappointed when she woke up and realized she was alone. She smiled as she rolled onto her back, remembering the tender way Vic had held her while she fell asleep. God, was this really happening between the two of them? And had she actually agreed to be her date for Vanessa's wedding reception? What the hell had she been thinking?

"Obviously, I wasn't thinking," she muttered to herself as she got up and made her way to the bathroom. She smelled coffee and something else…cinnamon? Oh, yes, please let Megan have made her awesome cinnamon rolls. She made her way down the stairs and found Megan in the kitchen, just taking the scrumptious morsels out of the oven. "Have I told you lately that I love you?"

"As a matter of fact, no," Megan answered without looking at her. "I think the only time you do is when I make these. Coffee?"

"Please." Riley made herself comfortable at the kitchen table and waited for Megan to join her. She wondered whether or not to tell her Vic had spent the night. Part of her wanted to keep it just for herself for a little while longer, but that was assuming Megan hadn't run into her that morning. "So, I didn't hear you come in last night. What time did you get home?"

Megan's cheeks flushed a light shade of pink and she looked away for a moment. Riley smiled as realization dawned. She didn't say anything though, opting to wait and see if Megan would admit to it.

"It was late." Megan shrugged and took a sip of her coffee.

"Late?" Riley asked. "Or early?"

"What do you mean?"

"Oh, my God, you stayed out all night." Riley laughed at Megan's look of shock. "It's about damn time."

"What are you talking about?"

"You and Peter. You guys have been in love with each other forever. What took so long?"

"Um, he was married, if you remember." Megan apparently decided it was fruitless to deny it any longer. "We only saw each other once every few years when a reunion came around."

"So, he's not married now?"

"They separated a few months ago. He didn't want to tell me over the phone, so he waited until last night."

"Wait, you talk on the phone with him?" Riley was surprised. She thought Megan shared everything with her. "How often?"

"I don't know," Megan said. "A few times a month maybe?"

"You better not be moving out to California." Riley started to panic, but then made herself stop, because what good would it do? Sure, she'd never be able to afford this place on her own, but she could find something else. Hopefully.

"What difference does it make?" Megan grinned and held her gaze. "Maybe you'll be moving to New York City."

"Highly doubtful," Riley said with a snort.

"Uh-huh, I saw your girlfriend when I got home this morning."

"She's hardly my girlfriend." Riley took a bite of her pastry and closed her eyes to enjoy the flavors better. "God, these are so good."

"Not the way it looked last night," Megan said, laughing as she shook her head. "People were taking bets as to how long it would take for you to rip each other's clothes off."

"Shut up, they were not." Riley covered her face with her hands.

"It was a pretty hot and steamy few minutes there with you straddling her in front of everyone. I'm sure the whole town has heard about it by now."

"Well, for your information, there was no clothes ripping last night." Riley stood and got the coffee pot to refill their cups.

"I know. Vic told me this morning."

"You talked to her? About us?"

"I told her if she hurt you I'd go after her."

"What did she say?"

"She told me she's the one more likely to be hurt. She thinks when she goes back to the city she won't see you again unless she comes here." Megan watched her for a moment, and Riley knew she couldn't argue with what Vic had told Megan. She didn't travel, and that was pretty much the truth. "Please tell me you won't be like that. I've seen you involved with other women, and you've never been this happy with any of them. And you haven't even slept with her yet. Don't let her slip through your fingers because you refuse to travel."

"I can't promise anything," Riley said, shaking her head. She hated herself for worrying so much about her mother. Her mother had never shown one iota of concern for her after she'd started drinking, and Riley wished she could return the favor, but it wasn't in her nature to turn her back on anyone in trouble.

Not even the woman who only talked to her if she needed money.

CHAPTER SEVENTEEN

Riley was putting the finishing touches on the dinner she was making for Vic when the doorbell rang. She was early, but it didn't bother Riley at all. She wiped her hands on the dishtowel as she made her way to the front door, sporting what she was sure was a goofy grin. She pulled the door open and her face fell. It was her mother.

"Are you going to invite me in?" her mother asked, looking at her expectantly.

Riley wanted to tell her no, because she really didn't want her to be there when Vic was supposed to arrive in about twenty minutes. Instead, she stepped aside and motioned her in. Hopefully, this would be a quick visit.

"Why are you here?" Riley asked, irritated. "You never come over."

"Well, I haven't seen you for so long. Can't a mother visit her daughter once in a while?"

"I guess you've conveniently forgotten how you practically threw me out of your hospital room when you almost died of alcohol poisoning." Riley nearly slammed the front door before following her into the living room. "I don't even care why you told the hospital staff to never notify me when you were brought in. All I care about is that you *only* get in touch with me when you want money. So, let me save you the trouble. I don't have any."

Riley watched as her mother took a seat on the couch and sighed. Her eyes appeared focused and bright, so Riley assumed she hadn't started drinking yet today. Strange. Usually she started around noon or shortly thereafter. Riley sat in Megan's recliner and waited for her mother to get to the point of her visit.

"Why do you always assume I want something?" Her mother set her purse on the floor next to her feet and settled back into the couch. Riley decided not to say anything about her ignoring the comment about her being in the hospital. It wasn't worth it. Riley didn't offer her anything to drink because she didn't want her thinking she was welcome to stay any more than a few minutes.

"Because you do, and there's no use denying it." Riley looked at her phone to check the time and shook her head impatiently. Vic would be there soon, and she didn't think there was any way in hell she was going to avoid a face-to-face meeting between the two of them. "So just tell me what it is. I'm expecting company."

"Oh?" Her mother perked up at the news, and Riley regretted letting it slip. It seemed Megan had been right in assuming the entire town had heard about what happened at the reunion. You couldn't do anything in Wolf Bay without everyone knowing about it. "Victoria Thayer, I assume?"

"You need to leave. Now." Riley got to her feet and headed for the front door. "I'll call you tomorrow."

"Why wouldn't you tell your poor old mother you're dating such an attractive young woman?" Her mother hadn't moved, and Riley turned to look at her just as she heard a car door slam out front.

Shit.

Without a word, she stepped out onto the porch and pulled the door closed behind her. Vic looked surprised to see her standing there.

"I think I'm supposed to knock, or ring a bell or something, and *then* you answer the door." Vic grinned at her, and Riley couldn't stop her own smile from happening. Then she thought of her mother sitting in her living room. "Or were you just so excited to see me you couldn't wait?"

"Yeah, that's it," Riley said with a quick glance over her shoulder at the front door.

"Well, *that* sounds convincing."

"I'm sorry." Riley closed the distance between them and kissed her quickly on the lips. "My mother is here."

"Oh?" Vic looked surprised, but then must have remembered Riley's feelings about her mother. "Oh. Should I go?"

"Don't you dare. I just wanted to warn you. Trust me, she won't be staying long."

She led Vic into the house and straight on to the living room where her mother was still sitting on the couch.

"Mom, this is Vic."

"Please, call me Helen." Her mother stood and went to Vic, holding out her hand.

"Pleased to meet you, Helen." Riley could tell Vic's smile was forced as she shook the offered hand, but then she looked at Riley, probably hoping for some guidance.

"My mother was just leaving."

"No, I wasn't," her mother said with a laugh. She grabbed Vic by the arm and led her to the couch, pulling her down to sit next to her.

"Mom, Vic and I have plans."

"Well, you aren't going anywhere. I can smell the food cooking."

"Actually, Helen, I've asked Riley to accompany me to a party, so we have to kind of eat and run," Vic said, and Riley could have kissed her.

"Oh, well, I guess I should be going then." Her mother stood and ushered Riley into the kitchen. This was it. Riley knew she was going to ask for money. Riley went to the stove and leaned against the counter, waiting. "Honey, do you have a few dollars to spare? Just until I get my Social Security check next week."

"No, Mom, I don't. I never have any money to spare, so I don't know why you keep asking."

"What about your girlfriend? She's rich, isn't she?"

"I am not going to ask her to loan you money."

"But why not?"

"First of all, you won't ever pay it back, which is something I learned the hard way. And second, you'll only spend the money on booze. I won't do it."

"I've stopped drinking."

Riley let out a bark of laughter before composing herself again. She'd heard this declaration before, but her mother never followed through. It didn't stop Riley from hoping maybe this time she might truly mean it.

"I hope you have," she said with a slight nod. "But that doesn't change the fact I have no money to loan you."

"Couldn't you just ask her?"

"Good-bye, Mom."

Helen walked out of the kitchen muttering under her breath, but she stopped short as she rounded the corner and almost ran right into Vic. Vic had fully intended to follow them into the kitchen, but she stopped short when she heard Helen suggesting Riley ask her for money. Her heart was racing now, simply at the prospect of Riley actually doing it. Sure, she'd told her mother she wouldn't, but who knew what might happen after she had more time to think about it. Vic hoped she wasn't wrong in trusting Riley.

"Good-bye, Vic," Helen said before turning and walking out the door. A moment later, she was standing face-to-face with Riley, who looked nervously at the door then back to Vic.

"How much of that did you hear?" she asked.

"Enough." Vic fought to not confront her about what was said.

"Then you heard me tell her no." It was a statement rather than a question, and she placed her arms around Vic's neck.

"I did." Vic felt some of her apprehension melt away at her touch. She put her hands on Riley's hips and pulled her a little closer.

"I meant it when I said I didn't want your money, okay? And I sure as hell would never ask you for money for my mother. So, don't look like you want to bolt."

Vic smiled and nodded. God, how did Riley possess the ability to make her forget everything but the here and now? Whenever they were together, absolutely nothing mattered but that moment. She'd never experienced this particular reaction to anyone before and was a little surprised to find she quite liked it.

"I don't want to bolt," she said. "What I really want to do is get you naked. The sooner the better."

Riley slid her hands down to rest above Vic's breasts and playfully pushed her away. "You're here for dinner and a sunset. Nothing more."

"You can't blame a girl for trying."

"No, I guess you can't."

Vic pulled her flush against her body and moved her hands to Riley's ass. Riley melted into their kiss, and Vic was certain she wasn't alone in her desires, mostly by the way she allowed Vic's tongue past her lips so readily. The deep moan Riley let loose and the way her hands went to the back of Vic's head to keep her in place were also rather telling.

Riley looked dazed when she pulled away from her, breathing heavily as she licked her lips. Vic was sure the hunger she felt as she watched Riley's tongue was evident in her eyes.

"You don't play fair," Riley said, her voice raspy.

"Life isn't fair," Vic said with a wink, trying unsuccessfully to calm her racing heart.

"We should eat." Riley said the words, but she didn't make a move toward the kitchen right away. "I hope you meant it when you said meat loaf was okay."

"I'm sure anything you made will be wonderful."

"Ha!" Riley said as she finally turned and headed into the kitchen. "You say that now."

Dinner was indeed wonderful, although it wasn't meat loaf. Riley had made a roasted chicken with mashed potatoes and gravy, broccoli, and an amazing chocolate cheesecake for dessert. Vic ate more than she should have, but it had all been so delicious. She helped with the dishes even though Riley protested, and then they made their way up to the roof to watch the sunset.

"How would you feel about coming to visit me in the city?" Vic asked once they were settled, each with a glass of wine. Riley looked up at the sky but didn't say anything. Vic was pretty sure what her major concern was, and she sought to alleviate any uneasiness. "Just for a couple of days, because I know you're needed at work. And I have a guestroom, so there's no pressure to share a bed. Unless you want to. It just can't be the first two weeks I'm back, because I'm going to be swamped with Vanessa on her honeymoon and after being away for three weeks. My father is the boss, and honestly, he's advocating for this." She waved a hand between them, causing Riley to finally look at her. "So I'm pretty sure he'd be okay with me taking some time off if you came to visit."

"Sounds like you have it all figured out." Riley gave her a tight smile.

"I just don't want this to end when I leave." Vic spoke quietly, feeling as if she were to say the words too loud, they might actually come true. "I really do enjoy spending time with you, Riley, and I'd like to see where this might go between us. Please tell me you want the same thing."

Riley was still smiling, but it didn't reach her eyes which caused a little concern for Vic. Riley looked like she wanted to say something, so Vic decided to wait her out. Besides, she felt she'd already rambled on enough.

"Ask me again after the wedding reception, okay?"

"Okay," Vic said around the lump in her throat. She had the distinct feeling the reception might be the last time she ever saw Riley, and it actually made her heart hurt.

CHAPTER EIGHTEEN

The next two weeks flew by for Riley, which didn't really surprise her. After the dinner and sunset they'd shared, Vic had left with a simple kiss good night. The following Sunday and Monday, they'd gone out to dinner, once in Albany, and once at the diner in town again. Vic had come by the theater to see her a few times, and they'd spoken on the phone daily. Now here it was, the night before Vanessa's wedding, and she was already regretting having to say good-bye to Vic after the reception.

"Riley," said Nancy as she stuck her head in the office. "The bachelorette party just pulled up outside."

Riley nodded at her as she felt her chest tighten. She wanted so badly to see Vic again, but she knew her heart was going to break when she left town in less than forty-eight hours. She stood and tried to straighten her hair and clothes before heading out to the front doors to greet the party. Well, to greet Vanessa, anyway, since the party was for her.

Vic and Vanessa were the last two to walk in, and Riley smiled slightly when she saw Vanessa was blindfolded. Vic met her eyes and gave her a big smile.

"Vic, where are we?" Vanessa asked. She sniffed at the air and Riley knew she would recognize the distinctive smell of a theater. Vanessa grabbed Vic's arm and turned toward her. "Oh, my God, I smell popcorn. I love popcorn. Are we seeing a movie?"

Riley almost laughed when Vanessa scrunched her nose up, because she was no doubt thinking the same thing Riley had. A movie theater was definitely an odd choice of venue to hold a bachelorette party.

"We are," Vic said as she removed the blindfold. Vanessa blinked a few times as she took in her surroundings. Her eyes stopped at the sign above the nearest theater door, then looked at Vic again with one eyebrow raised.

"Have you noticed they're only playing kid's movies?"

"On that screen, yes, but there are two other screens," Riley said, and Vanessa looked at her for the first time.

"Riley scored a copy of *Fifty Shades of Grey* for you," Vic said with a grateful smile directed at Riley, who felt something in her chest melt.

"Are you kidding me?" Vanessa practically screamed the words, and when Riley nodded in response, Vanessa threw her arms around her and squeezed her tightly. Vic met her eyes over Vanessa's shoulder and held a hand out for Riley, who gripped it without hesitation. "You're awesome."

"She is that," Vic said with a grin.

"All right, ladies, the movie will start whenever you're all ready." Riley spoke loudly as she made her way behind the snack bar counter and held her arms out to her sides. "Refreshments have already been paid for, so just let us know what you want. Unfortunately, we don't have a liquor license, so no alcoholic beverages are allowed."

A few women booed good-naturedly, and for the next few minutes they were slammed with orders for popcorn, candy, pretzel bites, and sodas. Once they were all inside the theater and settled in their seats, Riley ran upstairs and started the film. There were a few hoots and hollers as it began, but then they seemed to quiet down rather quickly to watch the movie. All but Vic, who Riley could see looking up at her.

She made her way back downstairs and found Vic waiting for her next to the box office. Vic motioned her over, so she told Nancy where she was going and headed her way.

"Can we talk outside for a moment?" Vic asked. Riley nodded and they headed out the door.

"What's up?" Riley asked as they stood next to each other, their backs against the wall.

"I wanted to make one more plea for you to come visit me in the city."

Riley looked away, nervous about having to address what might or might not be happening between them. "I would really like to come visit you, but I'm not sure when I'd be able to get away. Summer is usually our busiest time, what with the kids being out of school and all."

"Yeah, I get it," Vic said, looking more than a little disappointed. Riley allowed herself to be enveloped in a hug and they stood there holding each other for a few moments. "You're still coming to the reception tomorrow, right?"

"Just tell me what time, and I'll be there."

"Actually, I'll pick you up after the ceremony, around two." Vic took a step back. "The reception is at the house, so you're pretty much on the way from the church."

"You're sure you don't mind?"

"Not at all," Vic said with a smile and a shake of her head. "I'll see you tomorrow?"

Riley nodded and watched Vic go back to the theater. Her eyes were glued to Vic's tight ass, and just before she disappeared through the doors, Vic turned to look at her with a knowing grin. She was busted, and she totally didn't care.

❖

Riley finished all her work with about twenty minutes left before the last movie ended, so she decided to go into the bathroom to make sure there were plenty of paper products and soap for the next day. They had a cleaning crew that came every night after they closed, but she'd always liked to check those things herself. She noticed two of the stalls were occupied so she turned to leave.

"What the hell is Victoria doing with Riley Warren?" came a voice Riley recognized as Harper Reynolds's, Vanessa's best friend from high school. She stopped in her tracks, unable to move. "I mean I get that they're both lesbians, but isn't there some kind of standard for a Thayer to uphold?"

"She's just having a bit of fun." Vanessa's voice. Riley knew she should leave. Now. She knew whatever she heard next wasn't going to give her a warm fuzzy feeling, but she couldn't get her feet to move. "Fun is all it ever is for Vic, you know? I honestly don't think she'll ever settle down with a woman. Our mother has certain expectations, and Vic knows it. She'll fall in line someday, get married, and probably have children."

"But *Riley*? Certainly she could do better." Harper sounded just as bitchy as she had twenty years ago, which surprised Riley. Harper was one of the members of that crew who was actually friendly toward her now. She brought her kids in for Saturday matinees on a regular basis. Riley was surprised at the hurt she felt when she heard the words.

"It isn't as though there's a big pool of lesbians to choose from in Wolf Bay." Vanessa laughed, and so did Harper. The next words she heard though, made her blood run cold.

"I'm pretty sure even the straight women would be up for a bit of fun with your sister, if you know what I mean."

A toilet flushed, and Riley was finally able to force her feet to move. She didn't stop until she was in the office with the door closed. She leaned against it and fought to not let the tears fall, but it was a losing battle. She slid down to the floor and covered her head with her arms, crying quietly.

How could she have been so fucking stupid? Of course Vic was only having fun with her. There was nothing meaningful there, even if Riley had tried to convince herself there was. It had been the same in high school. Her mother had told her the bullying she endured was "Just a bit of fun. Get over it." She wasn't so sure she could this time. This time her heart had gotten involved. God, at least she hadn't slept with her. She banged her head against the door once and looked up at the ceiling, forcing herself to stop crying.

She made the split decision that she would go to the reception with Vic as planned and act as though nothing was wrong. Then the next day Vic would leave, and she'd never have to see her again. No big deal. Just one more day to get through. She got to her feet and took a deep breath. She jumped when there was a knock on the door.

"Riley, the last movie is over," Nancy said. "Vic would like to talk to you."

"I'm too busy to talk, Nance," she called out after scrambling into her chair at the desk so it wouldn't sound like she was right by the door. "Tell her I'll see her tomorrow."

She heard murmurs on the other side of the door, then there was silence. She let out the breath she'd been holding and dropped her forehead to the desk in front of her. Just one more day.

CHAPTER NINETEEN

Vic had never been so happy to see a wedding ceremony come to an end. What a farce. Her parents—no, her mother—had been adamant about having a church wedding, even though they'd never gone to church a day in their lives. Churches made Vic antsy. She knew there was no good reason they should, but she'd just never felt comfortable in them. It felt as though she was being judged by a bunch of people she didn't even know. Or, in this case, by a bunch of people she *did* know.

She stuck around for the obligatory family and wedding party photos, but as soon as she had the chance, she took off for the parking lot and her car. Her mother had made some smart-ass remark before the ceremony about her looking like a groomsman since her tux was the same as theirs, but then her father had led Vera away and she hadn't spoken to her again. Her father, on the other hand, had commented on how good he thought she looked.

God, she couldn't wait to see Riley.

But then again, she was a little nervous about seeing her after the way the night before ended. She was trying to make herself believe Riley really had been in the middle of something and just didn't have the time to say good night to her. But there was a voice in the back of her head telling her something was off.

She looked at the house as she pulled into the driveway, half expecting Riley to be on her way out so Vic wouldn't have to go to the door, but there was no movement she could see. She walked to the front door, her heart pounding. It didn't help that she was still in her tux and it was close to ninety degrees outside. She used the back of her hand to wipe sweat from her face before knocking.

She started really getting nervous when no one answered the door right away. When it did finally open, she was surprised to see Megan standing there and not Riley.

"I'm here to take Riley to the wedding reception," she said when Megan only stared at her, her eyes narrowed somewhat. Vic shifted her weight from one foot to the other. "Is there something wrong?"

"Come in," Megan said as she turned and walked toward the living room, leaving the door for Vic to close behind her.

"Is she ready?"

"Sit for a minute," Megan said, patting the cushion next to her. "I want to ask you something."

Vic sat, but she felt warmer than she had outside despite the air conditioning of the house. She leaned forward, resting her forearms on her thighs. "Ask away."

"Are you a player?"

Vic almost laughed before she noticed the serious look on Megan's face, and she instinctually knew such a reaction would be a bad idea. She just stared at her, wondering what the hell was going on.

"It's a simple yes or no question, Vic," she said after a moment. "Either you are, or you aren't."

"No," Vic said. "Did someone tell her I was?"

"I don't know." Megan shrugged. She looked like she was being honest, but Vic couldn't shake the thought someone said something to Riley the night before. "I'm asking for me. As the best friend protector."

"Okay," Vic said, drawing the word out as she glanced toward the stairs. "Is she coming to the reception with me?"

"As far as I know. She's upstairs getting dressed."

Vic breathed a sigh of relief and nodded once.

"You sure you aren't a player?"

"If I was, I probably wouldn't still be hanging around," Vic said, feeling as though she needed to be on the defensive now. "I'm sure she's told you we haven't slept together."

"Well, you are leaving tomorrow," Megan pointed out.

"You know what?" Vic stood and began to pace in the small area in front of the coffee table. "I understand that you guys hate the person I was back in high school. I totally get that, and honestly, I hate her too. But I've changed. As I'm sure you and everyone else has as well. I'm not out to hurt anyone, least of all Riley. I've had feelings for her since high school, okay?"

"You told me that, too," Riley said as she walked up behind her. Vic turned to face her, startled. Riley shook her head. "I'm just not sure I believe you though."

"I don't know what I can say or do to convince you my interest in you in genuine." Vic wanted to reach out and touch her cheek but thought better of it and shoved her hands in her pockets instead. "Are you breaking our date?"

"No, I said I'd go, and I will. You'll be gone tomorrow, so let's go and have some fun." She turned and headed for the door. "Later, Megan."

They were silent on the ride to the house, and Vic thought she'd never felt more uncomfortable in her life. There were so many things she wanted to say, but she came to the conclusion the only possible way to prove to Riley she was being honest was to show her the journal she'd kept in high school. There was no guarantee she'd believe her even then, but Vic didn't know what else to do.

Her mother had hired a valet service to park everyone's cars, so Vic handed off her keys. For her mother, it wasn't enough to be having the reception at what most would consider a mansion dropped into the predominantly depressed community. Vera stopped at nothing to impress her peers. It wasn't as though she'd bothered to invite any of the people of Wolf Bay, other than the few Vanessa had insisted on having there. The ones who'd been in the wedding party. She sighed as she went to open the car door for Riley. At least she'd waited for her to do that simple thing. Maybe it was a good sign.

"I'm sure it was a beautiful ceremony," Riley said as they walked toward the front door arm in arm. "You look very handsome in your tuxedo."

"Thank you," Vic said as she looked again at the simple outfit Riley was wearing. She'd look good in anything, but the slacks she had on hugged her perfectly in all the right places, and the blouse was a light green, which really accentuated her hazel eyes. "You are, as always, very beautiful."

Riley smiled at her, and Vic finally felt some of the tension surrounding them slip away. She took a deep breath and stopped short of reaching for the doorknob to enter the house. She turned and faced Riley, taking her hands in hers and looking her in the eye.

"Just so you aren't caught off guard, my mother will no doubt be very standoffish with you. If we're lucky. If we aren't, she might actually be hostile toward you. Don't let it get to you, okay?" She did reach out then and brushed a lock of hair out of Riley's eyes. "I won't leave your side the entire time, I promise. Just know that my father is very happy you're going to be here, and he'll be on our side."

"Okay, that isn't at all daunting," Riley said with a chuckle. "Should I have brought my boxing gloves?"

"That might not have been a bad idea," Vic said with a wink as she opened the door and they walked in. It seemed as though there were people in every room, even though Vic knew the actual reception was being held in the backyard. They made their way through the house, stopping briefly to say hello to a few people Vic hadn't seen in years.

Her father saw them when they walked outside and smiled as he walked toward them. He hugged Vic and then looked at Riley, his smile huge. It made him look younger than his sixty-three years.

"You must be Riley," he said, taking her hand between both of his. "It's a pleasure to finally meet you. I'm Vic's father, Garret. Do you know many people here?"

"Dad, most of these people aren't from Wolf Bay," Vic said with an apologetic smile for Riley. "Hell, I don't know most of these people."

"I don't either, if I'm being honest. I'm not even sure your mother does. I think they're just on some great list she found of the best people to have at your party." He laughed, and Vic and Riley joined him. Vic didn't doubt he was right, at least to a certain degree. These were no doubt people who her mother wanted to look good in front of.

"Have you been hitting the open bar, Dad?" Vic asked with a playful nudge to his shoulder.

"Damn right. I'm paying for it, so why shouldn't I?" He leaned in closer so only the two of them could hear him. "And it's the only way I can deal with your mother at one of her parties."

"Are you saying she's difficult to deal with?" Riley asked.

"To say the least." He put his arm around Riley and squeezed gently. "If she gives you any problems, find me. I'll deal with her."

"Thanks, Dad," Vic said, seeing Vera heading toward them looking decidedly pissed off. "Here she comes now. I think we might go inside for a bit."

"They're going to be doing the toasts and cutting the cake and all that stupidity in about an hour, so don't stay gone too long."

Vic shook her head in amusement as he made his way back to where Vera had been sidelined by someone Vic didn't recognize.

"What's inside?" Riley asked when they were alone again.

"There's something I want to show you, upstairs in the room I had when I was younger."

"You're just trying to get me alone, aren't you?" Riley grinned, and Vic feigned shock at the suggestion.

"I would never use an ulterior motive to get you alone." She started leading her back inside, but then stopped and looked at her. "For future reference though, would that work?"

"No." Riley shrugged. "Maybe?"

CHAPTER TWENTY

R iley looked around the room they went into, marveling at how much it looked like the typical teenager's room, circa late nineties. There were posters on the walls, CDs on a shelf along with a few *Star Wars* action figures. There was one poster in particular that caught her attention, and she couldn't help but snicker.

"What?" Vic asked, sounding somewhat defensive.

"Seriously?" Riley raised an eyebrow. "Britney Spears?"

"What can I say?" Vic shrugged as her cheeks turned pink, and Riley thought it was adorable. "I was obsessed with her, but I had no clue why."

"And now you do?"

"Well, no, to be honest." Vic laughed. "I don't find her at all attractive. And I'm pretty sure she can't sing all that well without all the electronic enhancements to her voice."

"Thank God, I was beginning to question your judgment." Riley went back to looking at the mementos from Vic's youth.

"And what kinds of posters did you have in your room?" Vic asked, a teasing note to her tone.

"Whitney Houston," Riley said without looking at her.

"Definitely more attractive than Britney." Vic smiled when Riley turned around, wondering if she was being made fun of. "And there's no doubt she could sing a thousand times better."

"You were into *The Phantom Menace*, too, I see." Riley picked up an action figure of Darth Maul and looked at it more closely.

"Hello? Natalie Portman?" Vic looked at her like the reason should be obvious, which of course it was.

"Yeah, I'll have to agree with you on that one," Riley said as she tilted her head to look at the CDs it seemed everyone in their graduating class had been listening to. "So, what did you want to show me?"

Vic walked over to her desk and opened a drawer. She pulled out a notebook and opened it before looking at her again. She held it out to her, but she seemed reluctant to actually let her have it.

"You said you didn't believe I had feelings for you in high school," she said quietly. "I kept a journal our senior year. I want you to read this part."

"Are you sure?" Riley asked, surprised. "I never kept a journal, but I would imagine it's a pretty private thing."

"It is, and no one has ever read it before. But I want you to, because this part's about you."

Riley took it but never looked away from Vic's eyes. Vic sat on the edge of her bed and sighed. She looked so vulnerable, and Riley felt a fierce need to protect her despite her reluctance to trust in the things Vic said over the things she'd heard Vanessa say the night before.

"I don't have to," she said, shaking her head and trying to hand it back to her. Vic held up a hand to stop her.

"I really want you to."

Riley held her gaze for a moment and finally nodded once before sitting next to her. Her heart was pounding because she wasn't sure what she was going to read. She hoped it wasn't going to dredge up all those old feelings of being bullied. She took a deep breath and looked down at the notebook to start reading.

God, I am so over the way they're treating Riley Warren and her friends. Nobody deserves to be bullied like that. They're so cruel! Riley can't help it if she's poor and has to wear secondhand clothes to school. And as for her mother being a drunk? So not Riley's fault.

"Thank you for acknowledging it wasn't my fault that my mother drinks." Riley wasn't sure she wanted to keep reading. She really didn't want to relive the past.

"I wanted to tell you how I felt then, but you know the crowd I was hanging around with." Vic motioned for her to continue, so she did.

But what I hate the most is when they call her a dyke and a lesbo. I tried to come to her defense yesterday, but then they just started calling me those names. It bothers me that it bothers me, you know? But then I think, what if I am? I know I shouldn't give a fuck what anyone thinks of me, but I do care what Vanessa thinks. She's so disgusted by the mere possibility someone in our school might be gay—how would she react if her own twin sister was?

Riley stopped again and looked at Vic. She shook her head and reached for her hand. After bringing it to her lips briefly she held it in her lap.

"I had no idea they made you feel like this about yourself, Vic. God, I wish you'd felt like you could have talked to me about it. It might have changed things. For both of us."

"Keep reading. You might not feel that way after you see what's next." Vic smiled to soften her words, and Riley chuckled, figuring she already knew what was coming next.

So, I can't be a lesbian. But God, Riley confuses the hell out of me. I see her in the halls, and all I want to do is be near her. I sit next to her in English, and all I can think is how good she looks and smells, and I want to be even closer than our desks allow. My heart races, and my palms sweat, and I can't stop thinking about her. I think I want to kiss her, but then I realize kissing would never be enough. Damn it, I can't wait for graduation, and then I can get out of this shit town and be away from her. Away from the one person I know I'll never be able to have.

Riley closed the notebook before roughly wiping the tears from her cheeks. How was it possible Vic had been having the exact same feelings Riley had back then? Jesus, so much time wasted. She turned her head to look at Vic, but she was staring straight ahead, a couple tears of her own on her cheek. Riley gently brushed them away before putting her fingers under Vic's chin and forcing her to look at her.

"I wish you'd told me," she said, her voice strangled.

"I wish I'd had the nerve to," Vic said with a shrug. "I was never honest with myself about how I felt until I wrote that down, and I had my head up my ass about it all until I went off to college."

"You could have had me." Riley nodded and smiled. "You definitely could have had me."

"If I only knew then what I know now."

She leaned in to kiss her, and Riley let her. But when Vic tried to push her onto her back, Riley moved away from her.

"I'm not doing this here," she said. "Your mother could walk in any minute."

"Then she'd get what she deserves for not knocking first," Vic told her. She groaned when Riley stood and went to place the notebook back in the drawer.

"Come on, we don't want to miss the whole party, or they're going to think we're doing that anyway." She walked toward the door, but Vic grabbed her around the waist before she could open it.

"You have no idea how much I want you right now," Vic said into her ear before her tongue moved along the rim, causing a shiver to run through Riley.

"I think I might," she said, turning in her arms to kiss her. It ended too soon when the door opened, and Vera Thayer was standing there.

"What the hell is going on here?" she shrieked, looking horrified. "I want you both out of my house right now!"

"Chill out, Vera," Vic said, and Riley tried her best not to laugh at the absurdity of it all. "It was only a kiss."

"Don't tell me to chill out, and when did you start calling me Vera?"

"Don't try to save face, Vera. You know I started calling you that when you made it clear I was no longer your daughter." Vic took Riley by the hand and led her out to the hallway. "And we're not leaving unless Vanessa tells us to. Or have you forgotten this is her day, and not yours?"

They left her sputtering and hurried down the stairs before they both broke out in uncontrollable laughter. Riley glanced back up, almost expecting her to be running after them with her hair on fire. She couldn't believe the woman really had just walked into the room without knocking. She was glad she'd stopped what would have surely been a much more embarrassing situation.

"What's so funny?" Vanessa asked, walking up to them. "Come on, share."

"Vera caught us kissing," Vic said when she'd stopped laughing long enough to get the words out. "She wants us out of her house, but I told her we weren't going unless you told us to."

"You aren't going anywhere," Vanessa said before she switched her gaze to Riley. "Neither of you are going anywhere. She caught you kissing? Where?"

"In the bedroom." Vic looked at Riley and seemed as if she might start laughing again.

"Serves her right for not knocking."

"Exactly what I said."

"Come on," Vanessa said as she threaded her arms in both Vic's and Riley's as she turned them toward the door leading to the backyard. "The festivities are going to start soon."

"I hope you don't mind," Vic said, looking around her sister to see Riley. "I put you in for the filet mignon and lobster tail for dinner."

"Lobster again?" Riley asked with a grin. "You're going to spoil me."

Vanessa and Vic shared a look that Riley couldn't decipher, and she had the feeling she'd said the wrong thing. Vic smiled at her, but it seemed forced to Riley. She tried to push it from her mind and allowed herself to be led into the backyard. Vanessa left them at the table in front, facing the long table set up for the bride and groom and their parents. Riley found the placard with her name on it and began to sit, but Vic was right there.

"Allow me," she said, pulling the chair out for her. Once seated, Vic leaned down to speak into her ear. "You really are beautiful today. Promise you'll dance only with me."

"I promise," she said, directing her gaze to Vic as she sat in the chair next to her. She wasn't entirely sure she even wanted to dance, but when Vic looked at her that way, she was pretty sure she wouldn't be able to deny her anything.

CHAPTER TWENTY-ONE

Dinner was amazing, which didn't really surprise Vic. Vera would never serve anything to her guests but the very best. And the most expensive. Vera gave the speech that should have been Vic's to give, but she hadn't wanted to stand up in front of all these people anyway, so she didn't put up much of a fight when Vera announced her intentions. So, they sat through all the speeches and, at some point, she'd reached under the table to hold Riley's hand. Since Riley didn't object, she'd left it there until it was time for the cake cutting, and then dessert.

She watched Vanessa dance with their father, and Vic couldn't help the swell of love she felt for them both. He seemed genuinely happy for Vanessa. He'd always claimed Vanessa was the baby since she'd been born twenty minutes after Vic, so therefore Vanessa was his little girl. Vic didn't mind it though because she'd always been his firstborn.

She was lost in her thoughts when Riley squeezed her hand to get her attention. Vic looked up and saw Vanessa was motioning for them to join in on the dancing. She couldn't believe she'd missed the end of the father-daughter dance and the beginning of the bride and groom's first dance. She stood and held her hand out for Riley who smiled as she took it.

It was a slow song, so when they stopped next to Vanessa and Martin, she turned and took Riley into her arms. She heard people murmuring, but she really didn't care. She had a gorgeous woman in her arms, and it was the happiest day of her sister's life. Of course, the loudly screamed *oh, my God* got everyone's attention, and they all stopped what they were doing. Vic wasn't shocked to see it had been Vera, and she was being held by her father.

"What a fucking drama queen," Vic said, loud enough for only the four of them to hear it.

"She's done everything in her power to take the spotlight away from us today," Vanessa said, shaking her head. She placed a hand on her new husband's cheek and gazed into his eyes.

"At least she isn't going on our honeymoon with us." He laughed, but Vic and Vanessa looked at each other. "Wait, she isn't, right?"

"No, dear," Vanessa said. "You're stuck with just me for the next two weeks."

"Thank God. You had me worried for a minute."

"Just don't be surprised if she shows up at some point though," Vic said, somehow managing to keep a straight face. He looked horrified.

"Relax, she's kidding," Vanessa said.

Vic turned her attention back to Riley and smiled at her. They moved slowly to the music, and Vic loved the way Riley's body felt pressed tightly against hers. If only they weren't in front of a crowd of people.

People danced well into the evening, and Riley had kept her promise to dance only with her. Well, except for the one song her father somehow managed to finagle. Vic didn't mind because he talked to Riley through the entire dance, and even made her laugh at one point. Why couldn't Vera be more like him? Vic glanced over at her, still at the main table, and saw she was glaring at her. Vic refused to be goaded into anything. She waved at her and turned to Vanessa when she touched her arm.

"We're leaving soon."

"God, no, don't leave me here with her," Vic pleaded.

"Daddy will be here," Vanessa said with a swat on her arm. "He'll protect you. He seems pretty taken with Riley."

"He does, doesn't he?"

"She makes you happy, doesn't she?" Vanessa looked her in the eye, and Vic nodded. "But don't forget, your place is in the city, not here canoodling with her."

"Again with the canoodling?" Vic laughed. She saw Martin looking their way and she nudged Vanessa toward him. "I think your husband is trying to get your attention. Have fun on your honeymoon. Don't do anything I wouldn't do."

"I can tell you right now I'll be having sex with him, and I know that's something you wouldn't do, so I won't make that promise." Vanessa hugged her tightly then let go and stepped back.

"Yeah, I guess I can't expect you to." Vic kissed her on the cheek. "Don't forget to send lots of postcards."

"Not gonna happen. I'll be otherwise engaged."

Vic just laughed as she watched her go to her husband and then she sighed. It had never occurred to her before this moment she was actually going to have to share Vanessa with someone. The realization made her a little sad. Yeah, she and Martin had been dating for some time, but they didn't live together, so that left plenty of time for her and Vanessa to still see each other away from work most of the time.

"You look like you just lost your best friend," Riley said as Vic felt her hand slide into hers.

"No, I've gained a pretty awesome brother-in-law." Vic smiled as she looked at her. "You want to dance some more?"

"I think I'm all danced out. Take me home?"

Vic nodded, wishing it was something she could hear Riley ask her more than this one time. She glanced around for her father and was disheartened when she saw him back at Vera's side. She sighed.

"Just let me go tell my father I'm giving you a ride," she said. "Come with me?"

She walked up behind her father and placed a hand on his shoulder. He turned to look at her and smiled as he covered her hand. She glanced at Vera before leaning closer to him.

"Riley's ready to go, so I'm going to take her home now. I'll be back to have a night cap with you."

"No, you will not," Vera said with so much venom Vic actually took a step back. "You were only here for Vanessa, and now that she's gone, so are you."

"Vera, she's leaving in the morning, isn't that soon enough?" her father asked.

"You have no idea what I caught them doing." Vera looked thoroughly disgusted as she shook her head. "I want her gone now."

"It's all right," Vic said with a quick squeeze to his shoulder. "I'll see you Tuesday morning at the office."

"This is your home too, Vic," he said, directing an angry look at Vera. "You will not be made to feel unwelcome here."

"You have to pick your battles, you taught me that." Vic shot a look at Vera as well. "This one isn't worth fighting. It never has been. And honestly, I've felt unwelcome here since before I left for college. Why do you think I never came back?"

She turned without another word and took Riley's hand, leading her back into the house. She heard her parents arguing as they walked away, but she tuned it out. It felt good to have her father fighting for her, but she had no desire to hear anything else Vera had to say about her.

"Are you okay?" Riley asked as they walked into her bedroom again. Vic didn't like the look of unease on her face and forced a smile and a nod.

"Fine. I just need you to wait for a few minutes while I get my things." She moved around the room, picking up any stray items she may have left behind. She'd done most of her packing the night before, knowing she'd be leaving first thing Monday, so it was really only toiletries she needed to grab.

"No problem," Riley said as she took a seat on the edge of the bed. "Where are you going to stay tonight?"

"I'll probably just start back toward the city," Vic answered with a shrug. She shoved the last of her things in a bag and stood before Riley. She wanted to go back down and scream at Vera, and as good as that might feel, she knew it would accomplish nothing, so she was trying her hardest to calm her racing heart and her anger. "I'll stop at a hotel somewhere since it's getting a bit late."

"You could stay the night with me." Riley seemed as surprised as Vic was at the words. Vic shook her head and started to speak, but Riley stopped her by standing and placing a hand on her chest, just below her collarbone. "You've had a few drinks, Vic, and I'd hate for you to get into an accident. We'll get an Uber, and you can stay with me tonight."

"Only if you're sure?" Vic hated feeling insecure, but she never really knew what Riley was thinking or feeling from one minute to the next. She hadn't felt this way since she was eighteen, and it was unnerving. "Will Megan be okay with me being there?"

"She's working overnight, so she won't even be there. And yes, I'm sure."

"Then let's go," Vic said before placing a kiss on her lips. Riley started to reach for the big suitcase, but Vic handed her the smaller bag containing her toiletries instead.

"It was a nice party," Riley said as they settled in on the couch next to each other, their thighs touching. They each had a glass of wine and Riley had the television remote in her hand.

"Yeah, it was," Vic said in agreement. "Even though Vera had those people there for her and not really for Vanessa."

"What do you mean?" Riley hadn't believed Vic's depiction of her mother being such a snob, but now she'd experienced it firsthand. Her own mother was bad, but Vera took bad motherhood to new levels.

"I bet Vanessa didn't know more than ten people there."

"Are you serious?" Riley was truly surprised. "There had to have been more than a hundred."

"It isn't just you Vera doesn't like," Vic said. "She wouldn't invite anyone from Wolf Bay if her life depended on it."

"Then why does she still live here?"

"She loves the house and the gardens, and the prestige it brings her when she has parties like this one." Vic took a drink of her wine before setting the glass on the coffee table. "She allowed Vanessa to invite two people from town who weren't in the wedding party. The rest of the guests she knew were relatives."

"Are you serious?" Riley asked again, knowing she sounded like a broken record. Vera really was a world class bitch. "Why did Vanessa let her do it?"

"Nobody *lets* Vera do anything." She chuckled, but Riley was certain there was no humor behind it. "You know what? I really don't want to talk about my mother anymore if that's all right with you."

"Yeah, of course," Riley said. "The more you tell me about her the more pissed off I'm getting anyway. What should we talk about?"

"You coming to visit me in the city," Vic said, turning so she was facing Riley. "Like I said before, I have an extra bedroom, so there wouldn't be any pressure. I just don't want to leave tomorrow and feel like the only way I can see you again is to come back here."

"What are we doing, Vic?"

"What do you mean?"

"What's happening between us?" Riley's heart was beating so fast she worried she might pass out. She wanted so much for this to turn into something more, but what could she possibly offer someone like Victoria Thayer?

"I'm not sure, but I know I don't want it to end," Vic said, sounding genuine, but Riley was still skeptical. "I realize we don't know each other very well, but I'm really hoping that's going to change."

"Why? I mean, there are so many women to choose from in the city, I'm sure," Riley said, looking away. "What can you possibly see in me?"

"Are you kidding me?" Vic said, taking Riley's hand in hers and bringing it to her lips. "You're beautiful, you make me laugh, and after spending this time with you over the past few weeks, I honestly can't imagine not having you in my life."

"But I have nothing to offer you, Vic," she said, shaking her head. "I'm trailer trash, remember? You'd be better off with a woman who doesn't bring so much baggage to a relationship."

"Trust me, I have baggage too. And I don't want any other woman, Riley, I want you," Vic said softly. Riley looked at her then, and immediately wished she hadn't. There was so much emotion swirling in Vic's eyes it threatened to overwhelm her. Vic placed a hand on her cheek and ran her thumb along Riley's lower lip. "Can't you see that?"

Riley didn't resist the pull between them, and they leaned toward each other until their lips touched. She opened her mouth when Vic's tongue demanded entry, and she melted as their tongues slid together. She gripped her neck to hold her where she was, and Vic's hands moved underneath her blouse, stopping when they reached her breasts.

"I want to make love to you, Riley." Vic brushed a thumb over the material of the bra covering Riley's nipples, causing her to surge against her. "Will you let me?"

Riley turned her head away, needing air and a little distance to clear her head. Even though she wanted this more than she'd dreamed possible, it didn't feel right. Not with Vic leaving in the morning. When she felt she had a handle on her emotions, she looked into her eyes, a hand on her cheek.

"I want that too," she said. "But I don't want it to be on a night when you're leaving. If it happens..."

"If?" Vic asked, looking worried.

"*When* it happens," Riley amended with a slight smile. "I want it to be a night where I know I'll be able to keep you in bed with me the entire next day."

"Does that mean you'll come visit?" Riley laughed at the hopeful look Vic gave her.

"I can't promise when, but yes, I'll come visit if you really want me to."

"Of course I do," Vic said, resituating so there was a bit of distance between them. "You're killing me, but I can wait."

Riley smiled, thinking how easy it would be to fall in love with her.

She wasn't entirely sure she hadn't fallen already.

CHAPTER TWENTY-TWO

When Riley hadn't heard from Vic a week after she'd left, she decided to send her a text, just to let her know she was thinking about her. She'd responded quickly, telling her she missed her, but then there was nothing else. At all. Another week passed with no communication from her, and Riley was starting to wonder if she'd imagined it all. Maybe it really had been too good to be true.

"You seriously need to cheer the hell up," Megan said one morning. "You're starting to bring me down."

"Why hasn't she called?"

"I can't answer that." Megan poured them both a cup of coffee and joined her at the table. "Maybe she's just crazy busy. Have you tried calling her?"

"No, but is she too busy to make a phone call?" Riley shook her head. "She's probably found someone new already."

"Please," Megan said with a wave of her hand. "I know I'm not the brightest bulb in the pack, but I truly believe she's crazy about you."

"Or I was just a nice distraction from her insane mother while she was stuck in town for her sister's wedding. I need to wise up, Megan," she said, sitting up straighter. "She's better off without me. I'm still that same loser I was in high school."

"Jesus, you have such a fatalistic attitude. Maybe, and I know I'm going out on a limb here, but just maybe she's been doing her job *and* Vanessa's while she's been away on her honeymoon. They do both work at the Thayer Group, yes?"

"Yes," Riley said with a slump to her shoulders. Of course, that was probably what was happening. But a part of her wanted to still feel as though Vic had moved on, because it might not hurt so much when she found out it was true. "Maybe you're right."

"If you're so worried, call her. I'm telling you though, you're going to feel like an idiot when you find out I'm right."

"Vanessa's supposed to be back today I think, so if she doesn't call in the next couple of days, I will," Riley said, grabbing a bowl and some cereal. "And I hope you are right. How's Peter doing?"

"He's coming to visit next week, so it might be a good time for you to make yourself scarce, wink-wink," Megan said with a grin.

"Wow, it must be serious if he's coming here. He said he'd never come back to this shit-hole just to visit." Riley poured some milk into her bowl and sat down again. "I'm really happy for you both."

"Thanks."

Riley ate her cereal and contemplated life without Vic. It was crazy, really, to think just a month ago Vic wasn't someone she ever gave much thought to, and now, it hurt her heart to realize she might have lost her.

"Welcome home, Vanessa," Vic said as she walked into her office and gave her a big hug. "Are you still happily married, or are you ready to divorce him?"

"Blissfully happy," Vanessa said with a grin. "Greece was amazing, at least what I saw of it. You know, we spent way too much time in our room."

"Yeah, I don't need to hear all the gory details." Vic laughed and took a seat on the couch. She looked around the office that was decorated so much more personally than her own was. Vanessa was happy in her job, and it showed in the décor. Vic, on the other hand, was tired of working for the family business. It wasn't what she'd dreamt of while growing up, but it had been expected.

"How was it while I was gone?"

"Hectic. I feel like I didn't have a second to myself. I'm ready for a permanent vacation."

"You should take one," Vanessa said with a nod, obviously not having heard the word *permanent*. "It does wonders to recharge the batteries, you know?"

"Yeah," Vic said with a sigh, deciding to let it go. By her calculations, Vanessa would realize what she'd said before the end of the day. She'd never have believed it possible, but she didn't feel like herself since she'd left Wolf Bay two weeks before. The time she'd spent in the town she couldn't wait to get out of twenty years ago had seemed to ground her. Or maybe it had been Riley. She couldn't really say. Maybe it had been the combination of the two.

"Vic, where are you?"

Vic looked up to see Vanessa watching her with a strange expression. Obviously, she'd zoned out, something she'd been doing with alarming frequency over the past two weeks.

"Sorry, what?"

"I asked if you've had any interesting dates lately," Vanessa said with another grin. "I miss hearing about your disasters."

"Maybe you missed the part about not having a second to myself?" Vic asked as she got to her feet. "And I'm glad you think my love life is so interesting."

"I'm sorry," Vanessa said with a frown. Vic waved her off and headed for the door. "At least you're away from Riley again. I'm sure that one wouldn't have ended well."

"What do you mean?" Vic tried not to sound defensive, but she wasn't sure she pulled it off.

"Well, you complain about the women you date only wanting your money. You know she does, especially with her background. I just think it's good that it's over."

Vic stared at her for a moment, not really sure what to say in response. She should just leave and not say anything, but her anger got the better of her.

"What the hell do you mean, 'with her background'?"

"She came from nothing, Vic, you know that. And working at a movie theater? Really? I'm sure she'd love to get her hooks in someone like you."

"For your information, she's the manager there, and she's actually hoping to buy the theater."

"Yeah?" Vanessa laughed. "With your money, no doubt."

"Jesus, when did you become so much like Vera?" Vic knew the barb would hurt Vanessa's feelings, but she couldn't really muster the energy to give a damn. She was already feeling guilty about having not called Riley, but she really hadn't had much time for anything other than working and sleeping. She refused to admit a part of her was worried about the very thing Vanessa was talking about. She was afraid she might be falling in love with Riley, and there was little else that mattered at the moment.

"What's your problem, Vic? You had your fun with her, and now it's time to get back to reality. Ooh, you should call Cybill. I know you both still have feelings for each other."

Vic left the office without a word, slamming the door behind her. Seriously? Cybill? Vic definitely *did not* have any feelings for Cybill other than total contempt. The woman had stolen money out of her bank account, for God's sake. She'd been so embarrassed by the entire ordeal that she hadn't even told Vanessa what had happened. She didn't stop walking until she reached her own office and locked the door. She sat at her desk and stared out the picture window, taking in the view of

Manhattan. She took the cell phone out of her pocket and scrolled to find Riley's number, hitting the number to call before giving herself the chance to change her mind.

"Hi, Vic," she said, sounding tentative, and Vic hated she'd had a part in making her feel that way.

"Hi," she replied, her heart feeling lighter than it had for days simply from hearing her voice. "I've really missed you, Riley. I'm sorry I haven't called, but with Vanessa being gone, I've been slammed with work."

"Oh, she's back already?"

"Today, yeah." She sighed, wanting so badly to see Riley, to touch her. She couldn't describe the feeling of emptiness she was experiencing and wasn't even sure Riley would understand it if she tried.

"That was a big sigh," Riley said with a quiet chuckle.

"I really have missed you," she said softly. "There were a couple of times I tried to call you, but got summoned to my father's office for meetings. Then I didn't want to call you while you were working, but I always fell asleep before I knew you'd be home. I swear it felt like I was working twenty-four hours a day."

"Well then, what are you doing next week?" Riley asked, and Vic's heart skipped a beat.

"Please tell me you're asking because you're planning to come to the city." Vic closed her eyes and actually crossed her fingers.

"If it's okay with you. If you're too busy I'll understand."

"I'll clear my calendar and take a few days off. When are you coming?"

"Can you take more days off after those weeks for the wedding?"

"Like I said, my father owns the company, so I have a little bit of pull," Vic said with a laugh. "Just let me know when."

"I could drive down Sunday morning and head back Thursday," Riley said. Vic heard her shuffling papers and she gave a fist pump to no one. "Unless you think you'll get tired of me after a day or two."

"Fat chance of that happening." Vic looked at her calendar and saw she'd have to reschedule a couple of meetings, but otherwise the week was relatively light with Vanessa being back. "I'm already counting the minutes until you arrive."

"Has anyone ever told you how charming you are?"

"No." Her father had told her on more than one occasion, but never a woman. Knowing Riley found her charming made her smile. "Maybe you bring it out in me."

"Maybe," Riley said, sounding thoughtful. "Text me your address and I'll be there Sunday."

When they hung up, Vic stood at her window and found herself smiling. She felt so good right then that she wasn't even pissed off at Vanessa anymore.

Well, maybe she wouldn't go quite that far.

CHAPTER TWENTY-THREE

Vic looked at the clock for what felt like the millionth time early Sunday afternoon, wondering when Riley would finally get there. The cleaning service had been there the day before, so she knew everything was spick-and-span, therefore she didn't know what to do with herself while she waited. She'd also had them make up the guest room—just in case. She didn't want to assume anything and figured it was better to be safe than sorry. She'd left Riley's name with the desk downstairs so she'd be allowed into the private elevator that would bring her to the penthouse.

She turned on the television but shut it off again soon after. There wasn't anything she wanted to watch, but she was tired of listening to her own voice in her head. She was about to put on some music when there was finally a knock at the door. She glanced around the place one last time to make sure nothing was out of place, then ran a hand through her hair before walking quickly to the door and pulling it open. She smiled at the site of Riley standing there with a suitcase in her hand. She didn't realize exactly how much she'd missed her until that very moment.

"Do you always open the door for just anyone?" Riley asked, one eyebrow arched.

"I never do," she replied, reaching for her suitcase and ushering her inside. Hers was the only residence on the floor, and for anyone to make it up this far, it was only because she'd left their name with the security team in the lobby. She was hesitant to hug Riley, because she wasn't sure where they stood after three weeks apart. Luckily, Riley didn't seem to be questioning anything and pulled her into a tight embrace as soon as she'd set the suitcase down. "God, I've missed you."

"Me too," Riley said before placing a kiss on her cheek and stepping back with a grin. "I was worried maybe you didn't want to see me again."

"I am so sorry about not getting in touch with you sooner. There really was no other reason than I simply didn't have the time." She gestured to a stool at the breakfast bar and moved into the kitchen. "Can I get you something to drink? I'm pretty sure I have just about anything you could possibly want."

"Grapefruit juice?"

"Um, no, and can I just say, gross. I hate the stuff."

"So do I. I was just testing your claim." Riley placed her arms on the counter and leaned forward. "I'll have whatever you're having."

Vic nodded before grabbing a couple of water bottles out of the fridge. She passed one over the counter to Riley and then stood there looking at her. "I can't believe you're actually here."

"I can't believe this place you live in." Riley turned on the swiveling stool and took it all in.

Vic glanced around, trying to see it as Riley might. Unfortunately, all she could see was a person with way too much money lived here. It was an open floor plan with a loft above where there were three bedrooms and three of the five bathrooms the penthouse held. There was another area up there that held a pool table and a fully stocked bar.

Floor to ceiling windows ran the entire length of one wall, and most of the adjoining wall. The view of the city was spectacular. The kitchen was fully equipped with top of the line appliances and cookware, which was wasted on her because she never cooked.

"It's a place to live," she said with a shrug before taking a drink of her water.

"Are you kidding me? This is amazing." Riley turned back to look at her and shook her head. "Give me a tour."

"Well," she said, motioning with her arm. "Here's the main floor, which as you can see holds the kitchen, dining area, and the living room. The door you see on the far wall leads to the bathroom on this floor."

"Bedrooms?"

"In the loft," she said, pointing upstairs. "Shall we go up?"

Riley nodded and jumped off the stool as Vic grabbed her suitcase again and headed for the stairs in the far corner. They made the trek up that led them to the pool table and bar, and Riley stopped to admire the setup.

"Wow," she said as she ran her hand along the edge of the table. "Do you do a lot of entertaining here?"

"No," Vic said with a shake of her head. "I honestly don't have a very big social circle. I shoot pool by myself once in a while, and Vanessa likes to play when she comes over. The fireplace up here has never been used."

She led Riley to the far end of the loft. "This is the guest bedroom," she said, opening the door and depositing her suitcase on the floor just inside. "Just so you know, you're more than welcome to stay in my room, but I had this one made up for you if it makes you more comfortable."

They looked at each other for a few moments, not saying anything. Vic waited breathlessly, knowing which choice she was hoping for, but wondering which way Riley was leaning.

"Why don't we see how the rest of the day goes before I make that decision?" she finally said.

"Sure, okay." Vic led her farther into the room and showed her the attached bathroom.

"Oh, my God, I think this shower is bigger than my entire bathroom at home," Riley said, staring in what Vic could only describe as awe. Vic watched as she went to the shower, opened the door, and ran her hand along the rough tile. "A rain showerhead? Impressive."

"Not as impressive as the one in the master bath," Vic said. "It has LED lights that change color depending on the temperature of the water. And it's at least twice as big as this one. They both have heated floors though."

"No way." She stared at her, mouth open. "Show me the master bath."

Vic chuckled and led her back across the open area to the master bedroom. There were floor to ceiling windows here too, and a king-size bed that seemed to catch Riley's attention. Vic watched her as she went to sit on the bed, Riley's smile a beautiful thing to see.

"Did you want to just sit there all day, or do you want to see the bathroom?" Vic chuckled as Riley got to her feet and followed her through the doorway into the bath. Riley stood frozen in place as she took in the entire thing. There were two shower heads in this one, and the room also housed a Jacuzzi tub along with a regular bathtub. There was a walk-in closet big enough to be a bedroom on its own off to one side.

"I love this place," Riley said softly. "I think I've died and gone to heaven."

"It's way too big, if I'm being totally honest," Vic said, feeling embarrassed. "I mean, who needs this much space?"

"Well, I would imagine you do since you bought it."

"Actually, my father bought it for me when I graduated from college. I told him then it was way too big for just me, but he said he hoped there would be a family someday."

"Did he know then that you were a lesbian?"

"Yes." Vic smiled at the memory. "He's always been on my side, no matter what. He said he knew I'd never have a husband, but I could someday have a wife and kids, and he said for him, there wasn't any difference. Family is family."

"Wow. What an awesome father."

"Yeah," Vic said with a nod. She allowed herself another moment of thinking about how wonderful hers was before turning to Riley. "Let's head back downstairs."

"Where does the other door lead?" Riley asked, pointing toward the only closed door left.

"It's another bedroom, but I don't have it set up for that."

"What do you use it for?"

"It's a studio," Vic said, a little embarrassed. She didn't tell many people she liked to paint. It was obvious Riley's interest was piqued. "I paint."

"That's so cool. Can I see?"

"Maybe later?" she asked, shifting her weight nervously from one foot to the other. "After I have a couple drinks in me, and it won't matter so much when you tell me how horrible I am."

"I doubt that will happen, but we can wait until later." Riley followed her toward the stairs again. "What are you going to make me for dinner in that fabulous kitchen of yours?"

"Nothing," Vic said, which caused Riley to grab her arm and stop her just before she started down the stairs. Vic shook her head with a sad smile. "I don't cook. Never learned."

"Then why on earth is your kitchen so up to date?"

"Vanessa always spent more time here than she did at her own place and insisted it all be redone because she loves to cook. I thought maybe we could just order a pizza or something and relax tonight. Unless you want to go out?"

"No, staying here with you sounds perfect, no matter what we eat."

"Really? Then I could go pick something up from McDonald's and you'd be good with that?"

"Yeah, maybe not," Riley said, shaking her head.

"I have take-out menus in the kitchen, so I'll let you decide what's for dinner."

The rest of the afternoon was split between watching movies and sitting to enjoy the view of the city. Vic told her about the plans she'd made for the week, including a stroll through Manhattan the next day since Riley had never been there, tickets to *Hamilton* on Broadway for Tuesday night and dinner at Gallagher's Steak House before the show, and an evening out with some of Vic's friends on Wednesday.

"I can't believe the view you have," Riley said when Vic rejoined her after ordering their pizza. "This really is amazing."

"It is, isn't it?" Vic looked out at the city, marveling at the fact it was just as awesome now as it had been when she first moved in fifteen years ago. But, if she was being honest, it had begun to lose a bit of its appeal for her in the past year or so. But seeing it with Riley by her side made it seem all the more incredible. She was tired of living in the city, and while she'd felt that way before spending time with Riley, it seemed to be losing its shine at a much more rapid rate since she'd returned from Wolf Bay.

"I don't think I'd ever leave the apartment if I lived here."

"But there's so much to do in the city," Vic said, reaching for her hand. "Shopping, dining, sports, and you wouldn't believe the movie theaters here. If you could own one of them, you'd make more money than you'd know what to do with."

"I'm sure." Riley laughed and squeezed her hand. "But since I'm also sure this penthouse is worth more than I'll see in my lifetime, I can only imagine what a movie theater would cost. Plus the fact they're all part of chains, it would never happen."

"Doesn't hurt to dream, does it?" Vic shrugged.

"I suppose not. I have rather perfected the art over the years."

"Did you bring your swimsuit?" Vic winced slightly at the obvious change of subject.

"This place has a pool, too?" Riley looked at her in disbelief.

"There's one downstairs on the third floor, yes, but I have a private pool."

"Where?" Riley lifted her feet and looked down. "Does the floor open up or something? Like the gymnasium in *It's a Wonderful Life?*"

Vic laughed and shook her head. It really would be so easy to fall in love with Riley. The thought should have given her pause, but the honesty of it made it seem so right. Why shouldn't she fall in love with her? Just because she didn't come from money?

"I didn't show you the best part of my living space here," Vic said as she stood and held a hand out to help Riley up. She held on tightly and led her to what Vic was sure she thought was a closet, but when she opened the door, there was an elevator waiting for them. Riley stopped in her tracks and looked around, obviously confused.

"What the hell?" she asked. "Does your penthouse apartment have a basement?"

"No, but it does have a roof." Vic walked in and waited for Riley before pushing the button to go up. "I was going to wait until it was dark out to show you this, but I couldn't wait."

Vic exited the elevator when the doors opened to reveal an incredible outdoor living space on the roof. Besides the pool, there was a state-of-the-art outdoor kitchen, a hot tub, and some lounge chairs set up under an awning. Riley looked completely in awe as she stood unmoving, still inside the elevator car. Her eyes were darting everywhere, and Vic simply smiled.

"Holy fuck," Riley finally said after a few moments. "Seriously, this is all yours?"

"All mine," Vic replied with a nod. "You like?"

"I *love*." Riley stumbled as she exited the car, no doubt realizing what she'd said. "Your penthouse, I mean. I love your penthouse."

Vic just nodded as she tried to suppress her grin. What she wouldn't give to hear Riley say she loved *her*. If she played her cards right, maybe someday she would.

CHAPTER TWENTY-FOUR

They brought the pizza up to the roof because damn, the view from there was just too amazing to not spend a few hours enjoying it. Riley couldn't believe the entire space, inside and out. There was even another full bathroom up here on the roof. She couldn't even begin to imagine how much the penthouse must have cost. She tilted her head back and gazed up at the sky.

"The view of the stars isn't nearly as breathtaking as it is from your roof. One of the downfalls of living in the city that never sleeps." Vic wiped her hands on a napkin before tossing it into the trash can a few feet away. She began to close the pizza box but stopped and glanced at her. "Did you want more?"

"God, no, I'm stuffed." Riley chuckled with a hand on her stomach. "Maybe for breakfast?"

"I love cold pizza for breakfast," Vic said with a grin.

"Really? I thought you might have champagne and caviar or something equally expensive." The look of hurt on Vic's face made her want to take the words back, but it was too late. She sucked in a breath and shook her head, but Vic spoke before she could manage to engage her brain.

"Is that what you think of me?" she asked quietly. "That I'm a spoiled rich bitch?"

"Vic, no, I was trying to be funny," she said, getting to her feet and going to stand in front of Vic's chair. She got on her knees and placed her hands on Vic's thighs as their eyes met. "I don't think of you that way, well, I used to a long time ago, but not now since I've gotten to know you. I really was just trying to be funny."

Vic stared at her for a moment, then broke into a wide grin. "You're adorable when your upset, did you know that? I was joking too, Riley. Honest."

"Bitch," Riley said with a playful slap to her leg. She stood again and was about to return to her own chair when Vic grabbed her hand and pulled her onto her lap. She immediately put her arms around Vic's neck and tossed her head back in laughter.

"Let's go for a swim," Vic said, nibbling at her ear and causing goose bumps to break out all over Riley's arms and legs.

"No swimsuit," Riley managed even though her breath was coming in short bursts.

"Who needs one?" Vic slapped her ass and pushed her off her lap. "I can shut the lights off so no one in the other buildings will be able to see a thing."

"I'm not skinny dipping with you," Riley said, hands on her hips.

"Why not?"

"You say no one would be able to see us, but how can you be sure?"

"Because I am," Vic said. She went to the elevator door where the light switches were located and shut all the lights off. It was completely dark on the roof, but Riley could see lights on in surrounding buildings. Vic came up behind her and slid her arms around her waist. Her lips were close enough to Riley's ear that she could feel her warm breath. "I promise no one will be able to see us."

Riley stopped Vic's hands when they went to the top of her shorts and started to pull down the zipper. She let her head fall back onto Vic's shoulder and sighed. God, she wanted this, but she felt uneasy stripping down to nothing on a roof in the center of New York City.

"Wait," she said, turning her head to nuzzle Vic's cheek. "The first time I see you naked, I want it to be in a bedroom, not on the rooftop."

"I have one of those too," Vic said, and Riley heard the smile in her voice.

"And there you go, flaunting your wealth," Riley said, turning in her arms. "I mean, who the hell can afford a rooftop pool *and* a bedroom?"

Vic laughed, a thoroughly enjoyable sound that Riley felt in the pit of her stomach. She stared into the blue eyes that seemed to be quite a bit darker than she'd ever seen them before, and her breath hitched. She wished she could trust the words Vic had said before, could trust her feelings were true, but something was still holding her back. She didn't think it was the conversation she'd overheard in the bathroom at the theater, but if she was being honest with herself, the things Vanessa said brought forth the fear she'd had since the beginning. What did she have to offer Vic, really? She shook her head and took a step back.

"Please don't pull away from me, Riley," Vic said, her voice not much more than a whisper. "I want you so much."

"Maybe it will happen this trip, or maybe it won't, but it isn't going to happen tonight." Riley ran a hand through her hair and put some more distance between them. "I'm sorry."

Vic just looked at her for a moment before closing her eyes and taking a deep breath. When she opened them again, she nodded once. She picked up the pizza box and turned to head for the elevator without a word.

"Are you okay with that?" Riley asked as she joined her in the elevator.

"I guess I have to be," she answered with a shrug. She smiled at her and sighed. "I'm a big girl. I can deal with it."

"You know I want you too, right?" They exited the car and made their way to the kitchen.

"I think I do, but your words are telling an entirely different story than your body is." Vic got out some foil to wrap up the leftover slices and then leaned against the counter to look at her.

"Please be patient just a little while longer." Riley was wavering, but she did her best not to let it show. Why the hell was she turning down something she'd wanted for as long as she could remember? How could she honestly expect Vic to understand when even she didn't?

"I'll wait as long as you need me to," Vic said, stepping toward her and pulling her close. "I would never force you to do anything you don't want to do, okay?"

"Thank you," Riley said. She allowed herself to be held for a few moments before pulling away again. "I think I'm going to get some sleep. Is that all right?"

Vic just nodded and Riley headed up the stairs to the guest bedroom where she sat on the edge of the bed, wondering what she was doing here. Vic had to have thought they were going to sleep together in spite of the offer for the guest room. Hell, Riley would have expected it too, had their roles been reversed.

On the drive here she'd convinced herself she was ready for it and had been prepared to share a bed with Vic, but then once she was here and she'd been shown the guest room first, she'd been relieved. It was almost as if the final decision had been made for her.

She wanted Vic—she had no doubt about that. The problem was in her own self-confidence. A woman like Vic had probably been with a lot of women. Riley felt inadequate. What if she couldn't please her? What if she turned out to be the worst sex of Vic's life? Riley fell back on the bed with a sigh and stared at the ceiling. Again, Wolf Bay was hardly a lesbian mecca. She could count the number of lovers she'd had on one hand, for God's sake.

She forced herself up and into the bathroom to brush her teeth and get ready for bed. She curled up on her side with a book in her hand, but after reading the same paragraph over and over, she put it on the nightstand and turned out the light. Sleep took its time claiming her, but she finally drifted off.

Vic put the wine glasses in the dishwasher and stood for a few minutes looking out at the city. Riley frustrated her no end. She wondered briefly if it was the challenge that was drawing her in, or if she genuinely had feelings for her. There was no doubt though, really. She was pretty sure she was falling in love with Riley. She'd never been in love before, so she didn't really know what it felt like, but that was just it. This didn't feel like anything she'd ever felt before. The need to be with her all the time. The desire to just sit and talk with her. Every other woman she'd ever been with had been all about mutual gratification.

While she wanted that desperately with Riley as well, it didn't seem to matter that Riley wasn't ready yet. Vic never thought she'd be okay with a situation like that, but she was. She knew in her heart it would happen eventually, so she was okay with waiting. The anticipation of it all was rather intoxicating if she was being honest.

She started up the stairs and pushed the button on the remote to turn off the lights as she went. She paused outside the guest room, listening, but there was no sound. She was probably already asleep. She rested her hand on the doorknob and closed her eyes. She fought the urge to open the door and finally let her hand drop to her side. She needed to respect Riley's boundaries.

She lay awake until well after midnight, unable to fall asleep knowing Riley was right across the hall. Vic wondered if she slept in the nude, or if she had cute little pajamas she wore. Since she'd slept in a T-shirt and shorts when Vic had stayed the night with her, it was probably likely it was either that or nude. The vision in her mind drew an exasperated groan from her throat.

Her body was on fire, and she knew she was wet just thinking about her. She turned on her side and punched her pillow in frustration. She closed her eyes, but then she could feel Riley's body pressed against her again, and they popped right open. More than once, she swung her legs over the edge of the bed and had to force herself to lie back down and *not* go across the hall and crawl into bed with her.

A couple of times she thought she'd heard Riley coming into her room, but when she'd look at the door it was still closed. Her mind was playing tricks on her. She finally turned on the television mounted to the far wall just to have some background noise so she wouldn't drive herself crazy with her own thoughts. Thankfully, it worked, and she soon fell asleep.

CHAPTER TWENTY-FIVE

Vic thoroughly enjoyed showing Riley the sights she'd never seen before, from the Empire State Building to the Statue of Liberty and Rockefeller Center. Times Square was a big hit with Riley too, as was the Museum of Modern Art. It had been a long day, but they'd both been so wound up from the excitement of it all, they managed to watch two Alfred Hitchcock movies before retiring for the night—in separate bedrooms again.

Tuesday was spent just hanging out at the penthouse until it was time to go for dinner, and then *Hamilton.* Vic had been to it before, but she thoroughly enjoyed watching Riley see it for the first time. Once back home, Vic offered a glass of wine and they settled into the couch to drink it.

"I want to thank you for the past two days," Riley said. She'd changed into shorts and a T-shirt after they'd gotten back, and she was sitting at the end of the couch with her legs tucked under her. "The show tonight was awesome."

"You're very welcome," Vic said with a nod. The urge to move closer and run her hand along Riley's calf was intense, but she was determined to allow Riley to set the pace. She wasn't going to push her. "I'm glad you had fun."

"Megan isn't going to believe it." Riley smiled and reached out with her foot to push on Vic's leg. "You seem to make everything fun."

"I do my best," Vic said, finally giving in to the desire to touch Riley since she left her foot pressed against her leg. She watched for any sign her touch wasn't welcome, but Riley allowed her to pull her foot onto her lap and she began to gently massage it.

"Oh, my God, that feels incredible," she said, leaning her head back and closing her eyes. Vic's breath hitched at the sight and she focused on the foot in her hands. "You have magic hands. Has anyone ever told you that?"

"No," Vic said with a chuckle. "But I'm glad you think so."

"I definitely do."

Vic took a chance and let her hands move up Riley's calf a bit and was surprised Riley again didn't stop her. The sounds she was making were slightly distracting, and Vic's breath began to quicken. When she was almost to Riley's knee, she realized Riley had fallen asleep. She sighed and lifted Riley's leg just enough so she could stand up. She grabbed a blanket and covered her with it before taking their wine glasses to the kitchen. She stood watching her for a moment, debating whether to wake her, but eventually decided to just let her sleep. She turned out the lights and went upstairs to her bedroom, entirely frustrated.

After a cold shower, she crawled into bed and stared at the ceiling for a few minutes before finally falling asleep. A noise woke her up around two in the morning, and she assumed it was just Riley finally making her way to her room. She started to fall back asleep when she felt someone sit on the other side of the bed.

"Riley?" she asked as she sat up and looked at her in the light that was coming from the windows. "Are you all right?"

"No, I'm not," she said, turning to look at her. Vic's heart raced.

"What happened? Do you need to go to the doctor?"

"I'm not sure a doctor would be able to help me with the problem I'm having."

"What is it, Riley?" Vic worried something was seriously wrong with her.

"Something only you can help with," Riley said as she stood and pulled her T-shirt over her head and let it drop to the floor. "I really need you to touch me, Vic."

Vic breathed a sigh of relief to learn she wasn't sick or injured, and it took a moment for her mind to catch up with what was happening. But when it did, she was instantly wide-awake. She pulled the covers back and held her hand out, waiting for Riley to take it. She did, after shedding her shorts so she was completely naked.

"Jesus," Vic murmured at the sight before her. Riley was perfect. So unlike the other women she'd been with, who only reached perfection through expensive surgical procedures. She mentally shook herself. She definitely did not want to be thinking about *anyone* else right now. Riley got under the covers and slid up against her.

"My, how convenient," she said with a chuckle as her hand rested on Vic's hip. "Do you always sleep in the nude?"

"Do you really want to discuss my sleeping attire right now?" Vic waited for an answer, which was a simple shake of Riley's head. Vic rolled them both over so she was on top of Riley, a position she'd dreamed about for weeks now. "Are you sure about this?"

Riley's answer was to wrap her legs around the backs of Vic's thighs and push herself up into her. Vic closed her eyes against the onslaught of emotions that washed over her with that simple move. When she opened them again, Riley was watching her breasts and her fingers moved to her nipples, squeezing gently.

"Fuck," Vic said under her breath. She pressed her pelvis against Riley, quickly realizing it wasn't nearly enough. She kissed Riley, a slow, sensual seduction meant to make her relax her hold on Vic's thighs that worked perfectly. Once free, Vic moved down her body, stopping to pay some attention to Riley's breasts. It was obvious they were a sensitive area for her when she moaned and tried to press against her again. Vic continued down across her navel and through the soft patch of hair between her legs before looking up at her. "Is this okay?"

"God, yes," Riley replied. She put a hand on the back of Vic's head and directed her to where she needed her. Her body tensed when Vic closed her lips around her clit, and then bucked when she began to suck on it.

Vic pulled away to gain better access and placed Riley's legs over her shoulders before focusing again on the beautiful sight before her. She slid her tongue inside Riley, causing her to moan loudly. She fucked her slowly for a moment before sliding her tongue through the wet folds back to her clit. She pushed two fingers inside her as she began sucking on her clit and Riley almost immediately tightened around her fingers.

"Yes, Vic, I'm coming." Riley screamed her name then and threaded her fingers through Vic's hair as she held her in place. After a few moments, breathing heavily and trying to push her away, Riley sighed. "Jesus, that was amazing."

"You're beautiful when you come," Vic said, moving so she was lying on her back next to Riley.

"Bullshit, nobody's beautiful when they come." Riley laughed and turned her head to look at her. "Just like nobody's beautiful when they cry."

"Well, you are," Vic smiled as their eyes met. "When you come, I mean, because, you know, I've never seen you cry."

"And I hope you never will," Riley said. She closed her eyes for a moment. "I'm sorry I woke you up."

Vic laughed and turned on her side, propping herself up on her elbow. She couldn't imagine a better reason for being awakened in the middle of the night. She ran the back of her fingers across Riley's cheek.

"Don't be, because trust me, I'm not sorry in the least."

"Good," Riley said as she placed a hand on her shoulder and forced her onto her back. "But we'll see if you still feel that way later tonight, because I don't plan on letting you sleep much more, if at all."

"I think I can live with that." Vic smiled before Riley kissed her soundly. She moaned when Riley's thigh slipped between her legs and pressed against her center. She knew she was wet, but the way she slid against her surprised even her.

"A little turned on, are we?" Riley cocked an eyebrow.

"More than a little," Vic said, putting her arms around her neck and pulling her in for another kiss. "You have no idea what you do to me, Riley."

"But I know what I *want* to do to you," Riley said with a lopsided smile. Vic jerked involuntarily when Riley pushed her hand between their bodies and began slowly stroking her clit. "Ticklish?"

"A little," Vic admitted and felt her cheeks flush. "Plus it's been a while since anyone's touched me like this."

"How long?" Riley looked surprised.

"About a year?" Vic said it like a question, even though she knew exactly how long it had been. It was the night before she threw her last attempt at a girlfriend—the infamous Cybill—out on her ass for stealing her money. Which had also coincided with the night of Vanessa's car accident in Wolf Bay. She hadn't had the desire to date since. Until now. Until Riley. She sighed.

"That's a shame," Riley said, her expression serious. She made a show of looking at Vic's body. "A woman like you should be touched as often as possible."

"You are more than welcome to do that yourself."

"I might take you up on that." Riley winked at her before moving to take a nipple between her lips, biting and sucking gently at first, but then harder as Vic's moans made it obvious she enjoyed what Riley was doing.

"I need you, Riley," she said, staring into her eyes, one hand on her cheek. Riley let go of the nipple and moved closer to her face. "I need you to make me come. We can go slow the rest of the night and explore each other thoroughly, but I really need to come. Now."

"I like a woman who knows what she wants and isn't afraid to ask for it," Riley said, chuckling. She moved so she settled between Vic's legs and looked up at her again. "Is this what you want?"

"Please." Vic nodded, and the moment Riley's tongue touched her swollen folds, she grabbed the sheet in both her fists and held on tight. It didn't take long, and Vic had known it wouldn't, based on how aroused she'd been ever since Riley arrived at her penthouse. She cried out her name and bucked underneath her, but Riley managed to somehow hold on and ride it out with her.

"Was that quick enough?" Riley asked, moving so she was next to her again.

"Perfect." Vic put an arm around her and pulled her closer so Riley placed her head on her shoulder. She kissed the top of her head and sighed contentedly. "You are perfect."

Riley began running her fingertips in a circular pattern over Vic's abdomen, slowly moving down toward her center. Vic felt her arousal building again and she couldn't help the moan that escaped her lips. She was definitely going to be tired the next day, and she really didn't give a damn.

CHAPTER TWENTY-SIX

Riley didn't want to go out with Vic's friends on her last night in the city. What she wanted more than anything was to just stay in bed with her until it was time for her to head home. She got the feeling Vic was reluctant to go out too, but she said she'd promised Vanessa she'd be there. Riley knew she should be completely sated—she'd lost count after orgasm number four—but she was fairly certain she'd never be able to get enough of Vic.

"We'll make it an early night, okay?" Vic said as they walked into the bar where they were to meet up with her friends. She leaned closer and spoke directly into Riley's ear. "I still have quite a few things I want to do with you, and they all require complete nakedness for us both."

"Jesus, you have to stop saying things like that." Riley felt her arousal ratchet up and she wanted to turn right around and leave, but Vic's friends had spotted them.

"We'll continue this later," Vic said with a grin before turning and waving back at them. As they approached, a beautiful woman strode quickly toward Vic and enveloped her in an embrace that was far too familiar for Riley's liking. When the woman proceeded to place a kiss on Vic's lips, Riley felt her stomach drop even though Vic was pushing the woman away. "What the hell, Cybill?"

"Oh, come on, baby," Cybill said, almost purring. "It's been far too long, hasn't it?"

"Funny, I was just thinking it hadn't been nearly long enough," Vic said, stepping back to take Riley's hand. Riley noted with satisfaction the look of indignation on Cybill's face as she eyed their clasped hands.

"Who's your latest plaything?" she asked, looking at Riley as though she were a piece of trash. Riley moved to take a step toward her, but Vic tightened her grip on her hand.

"This is Riley," she said, bringing her hand to her lips and meeting her eyes. "And she's no plaything, trust me. Riley, this is Cybill. My ex."

"Vic, we never officially broke up." Cybill pouted her displeasure, and Riley almost laughed at the expression.

"I threw you out on your ass, told you I never wanted to see you again, and had all of your things sent back to your apartment," Vic said, staring at her in what Riley could only describe as disbelief. "What about that struck you as not being official? Oh, and you owe me about two hundred thousand dollars, which I still haven't quite figured out how you managed to get out of my bank account."

Cybill turned on her heel and stomped away, stopping to say something to Vanessa before heading out the front door. Vanessa then came to stand next to Vic.

"I'm sorry, Vic," she said, looking a bit embarrassed. "Why didn't you ever tell me what happened? She stole money from you?"

"Did you invite her here tonight?" Vic asked.

"I did," said another woman who stepped forward and placed a kiss on Vic's cheek as she squeezed her arm. "I'm sorry. I didn't know what happened between the two of you. You really should keep your friends in the loop when it comes to things like that."

Vic hugged the woman and brushed her lips across her cheek. Riley began to wonder if Vic had slept with all of her friends at one time or another over the years. She wasn't normally a jealous person, but this evening wasn't starting out well.

"Riley, this is Tara," Vic said, turning to her.

"A pleasure," Tara said with a smile as she held a hand out. Riley took it, but Tara didn't let go. "Come with me to the bar to get a round for everyone."

Riley looked at Vic, who simply shrugged. Not wanting to cause a scene, Riley smiled and nodded at Tara.

"So, how long have you known Vic?" Tara asked as they waited at the bar to be served.

"Technically, we've known each other since grade school."

"Wow, really?" Tara seemed surprised, but Riley had the sinking feeling Vanessa had already filled them all in on Riley's past. "And how long have you been dating?"

"About six weeks." Riley looked over her shoulder and saw Vic being hugged by yet another beautiful woman. How could she ever hope to be able to keep her attention when it was becoming painfully obvious she was not Vic's type? Her heartrate kicked up, and it had nothing to do with arousal. That had been completely doused by now. She couldn't look away when she saw Vic lean in and say something in the woman's ear that caused her to laugh before she ran her hand down the length of Vic's arm and didn't stop until their fingers intertwined.

"Hmmm," Tara said with a slight smile. "That's about right, I guess."

"Pardon?" Riley redirected her attention to the woman standing next to her.

"Well, Vic never sticks with a woman for more than a couple of months, except for Cybill. And there's no shortage of women wanting to share her bed. You aren't her usual type though."

"No?" Riley asked, feeling her anger begin to rise. "Do tell."

"It's just…" Tara seemed to search for the words for a moment, then smiled again and shrugged. "Her usual type of woman comes from money. Or they at least have some type of standing in the business world. And more feminine, if you know what I mean. Like the woman she's getting all cozy with over there."

Riley just nodded, not trusting herself to speak as she looked back at Vic. She did indeed look rather comfortable with the woman who was holding her hand and seemed to laugh at everything Vic said. Riley's insecurities and self-doubt were beginning to rise to the surface, and she wasn't sure she'd be able to push them back down again.

"Tara, stop trying to scare the girl away," said the bartender as he placed a couple of coasters in front of them. He looked at Riley and shook his head. "Take it from Vic's gay best friend. These women will do whatever they can to chase you away. All they want is her money, and not one of them is a true friend. My name is Tyler, by the way."

"Hi, Tyler," she said. She knew his words should make her feel better, but her lack of self-confidence was too strong. "Riley."

"A pleasure to finally meet you, Riley," he said with a wide smile. "What can I get for you?"

She ordered a couple of glasses of wine for her and Vic, and Tara just laughed as though she'd made the biggest mistake of her life.

"Vic doesn't do wine, honey," she said, shaking her head and giving her a look of what appeared to be pity. She looked at Tyler. "Make that a brandy for Vic."

"How about I do both, and we'll let her decide which one she wants?" Tyler turned to get the wine from behind him and poured two glasses. He was muscular, which was obvious from the way his shirt fit him. His shoulders were broad, and his waist more narrow. His sandy blond hair fell into his eyes and he had a quick smile. Riley decided she liked him. He handed her the wine and turned to Tara, his smile disappearing. Riley took the wine and headed back toward Vic, but she stopped short of announcing her presence when she overheard the end of the conversation taking place.

"She's leaving tomorrow, so how about we have a drink and some dinner when you get done with work?" Vic said, her back to Riley.

"That sounds wonderful, Vic, I'll give you a call in the afternoon." The woman kissed Vic on the cheek before turning and walking toward Vanessa who was sitting at a table big enough for everyone present.

When Vic turned to face her, Riley noticed a slight blush to her cheeks. She hoped Vic wouldn't be able detect the slight tremor in her hand as she held out the wine.

"I see you met Tyler," Vic said with a tilt of her head toward the bar as she took the glass from her and sipped it. "He's my best friend."

"So he said."

"Tara didn't say anything to upset you, did she?" Riley forced a smile and shook her head. Vic didn't look convinced, but she didn't push it. "He doesn't usually announce he's my best friend."

"How's your wine?" Riley asked when she saw Tara was on her way back with her hands full.

"It's perfect." Vic smiled. She pulled a chair out for Riley, who sat next to Vanessa. Vic took the seat on the other side of Riley.

"Here's a brandy for you," Tara said as she set the glass in front of Vic with a wicked grin in Riley's direction.

"I'm good with this," Vic told her, pushing it away. She looked at Riley and scrunched her nose. "I never did like that crap. Probably because it was always Vera's drink of choice."

Riley felt a sliver of satisfaction when Tara seemed truly shocked at the declaration. She endured the small talk for a few moments, until Vic got up to go to the restroom. Tara followed her a few seconds later, and then Vanessa. That left Riley alone with the woman Vic had been a bit too familiar with earlier. They hadn't been introduced, but from the conversations going around at the table, she gathered her name was Lisa.

"So, you and Vic, huh?" Lisa said after a few seconds. Riley nodded, but said nothing. "You know she's bi, right? And she and Tyler are a thing?"

Even though Riley didn't believe it, the seeds of doubt had taken root, and she couldn't take any more. She stood without a word and left the bar, not stopping until she'd gotten to Vic's building and asked the valet to bring her car down. She gave the guy a ten-dollar bill she couldn't really afford to part with and got in the car, determined to make it home before she could change her mind.

Three hours later, she was at home, in her bed, crying for the first time in a long time. Vic had tried calling her numerous times when she was on the road, but she let it go to voice mail every time. And every time, Vic had left a message. She grabbed her phone and sent her a quick text letting her know she was all right and to just leave her alone, then she shut it off and tossed it onto the floor.

She knew she should have stayed and talked about it, but she just needed some time on her own to think things through. She wanted to believe Vic, and all of the things she'd told her, but the self-doubt had been taking hold since she'd been seven and her mother told her for the first of many times that she'd never amount to anything. That no one would ever love her. And that she'd never be happy.

She'd spent a lot of years trying to prove her mother wrong, but all it took to regress was a tiny bit of doubt being hammered home by multiple people. She was pretty amazed she'd made it through the entire ordeal without suffering a panic attack.

"Hey, Riley?" Megan said as she slowly opened her bedroom door and came in to sit on the bed next to her. "Sweetie, what's wrong? You weren't supposed to be home until tomorrow."

Riley told her everything, from how much fun they'd had together, and how it had all fallen apart in the span of about an hour. Megan held her, and Riley sobbed into her shoulder before finally falling asleep.

CHAPTER TWENTY-SEVEN

Vic was furious when Tyler told her the things Tara had been saying to Riley at the bar the night before. She'd told every woman there that she was through with them. It was something she should have done long ago. They were all so fake. And to top it all off, Riley had left without a word, apparently driving back home and out of her life. But there was no way Vic was going to give up so easily. She was in love with Riley. There was no point in denying the fact any longer, and she needed to make sure Riley knew it. She stepped off the elevator and headed straight for her father's office.

"Is he in?" she asked his assistant, Marie, as she walked past, not even slowing down.

"Yes," she said. "But he's in a meeting."

It didn't matter. Vic walked in the office without knocking and slammed the door behind her. Her father looked up in surprise, as did the three department heads who were seated around a small conference table with him.

"I need to talk to you," she said.

"Can't it wait? We're almost done here."

"No," Vic said with a quick head shake. She needed to do this. It was long overdue. She knew he would understand, and would no doubt be on her side. Unless Vera had gotten to him first. The thought threatened to make her lose what little breakfast she'd managed to eat that morning.

"It's all right, Garret," one of the men said. Vic didn't even know his name, but she knew he'd been with the Thayer Group for years. They began clearing off the table and stuffing things into their briefcases. "We can finish up after lunch."

The three men walked past her to the door, all of them giving her a smile and a quick nod. She realized she didn't know any of their names. It served to reinforce the knowledge she was doing the right thing. Her father picked up the phone on his desk and asked Marie to bring them a pot of coffee before motioning for Vic to take a seat. He took the chair next to her instead of sitting on the other side of his desk. He took her hand and waited for her to look at him.

"What's going on, Vic?" he asked, his voice full of concern. He'd always been able to tell when something serious was bothering her, and his compassion threatened to make her cry.

"I'm quitting." Vic stared at him, silently daring him to try to talk her out of it, but he hung his head and sighed.

"Okay," he said, giving her hand a squeeze before letting go. "I'll call HR this afternoon and have the paperwork drawn up."

"You aren't surprised." It was a statement more than a question, but he shook his head and met her eyes again.

"I've known for quite some time you aren't truly happy in this business," he said. "I'd hoped you might work through it, but if you want to leave, I won't stop you. Do you have something else lined up yet?"

"No."

"Then will you at least give us a two-week notice? I know we'll never find someone to do the job as well as you do, but will you agree to help train someone?"

"Of course," she said, never having been able to deny him anything. "Vera—"

"Don't worry about her." He stood and went to the windows to look out at the city. "I know she told you you'd be cut off if you ever left the company, but she doesn't make any of the business decisions. I had a fund set up for you *and* for Vanessa, in case this day ever came. You won't ever have to worry about money, I promise you that. Will you be staying in the city?"

"Honestly, if Riley will have me, I'll move back to Wolf Bay." Vic smiled when he turned around and looked at her, obviously surprised. She nodded. "I've fallen in love, Daddy, but I'm afraid it may be too late."

He sat next to her again and took both her hands in his. "If you truly love her, then you have to do everything you can to make it right. Do you understand me?"

"I didn't do anything wrong," she told him, her frustration at the situation rising. "It was a few people I thought were my friends who put ideas in her head."

"What happened?"

"She's not completely trusting where I'm concerned," she said, avoiding eye contact. Her father had been aware when she and Vanessa were younger that they had some type of involvement in bullying at school. He'd never been informed of the extent of it, and never knew who it was they were harassing. Vic took the time to tell him everything now, even how she'd been so confused about her sexuality and had tried to stand up for Riley.

"Well, shit," he said as he collapsed back against his chair when she was finished. "That kind of puts a whole new spin on things, doesn't it?"

"I've apologized to her for it, and I believe I've proven to her I'm not that person anymore, but that coupled with a neglectful and alcoholic mother has really damaged whatever self-esteem she might have had." She finally looked at him and wasn't really surprised to see sympathy in his eyes. She looked away again when she felt tears threaten.

"So how do you fix the problem now?" he asked.

"I think I need your help with that."

"I would do anything for you, Vic, you know that. Just tell me what you need."

❖

"I thought you weren't coming back until tonight," Nancy said when Riley arrived to open the theater Thursday morning.

"Change of plans," Riley said with a shrug as if it was no big deal. But it was a big deal. She knew she should answer the phone when Vic kept calling, but she simply needed some time to work through her issues on her own.

"Is everything okay?" Nancy asked, following her into the office and sitting with her. "Is it your mother?"

"What?" Riley was surprised by the question, but she shook her head. "No. I haven't seen or heard from her since the night she tried to crash my date with Vic."

"Then what is it, Riley?"

"Nothing." Riley sighed and looked up at the ceiling. "Just my own insecurities. I'll get everything sorted out. Don't worry about it."

"Hello, have you met me?" Nancy chuckled. "I can't help but worry about you. You're the daughter I never had."

"I love that you feel that way, Nancy," Riley said, meeting her eyes. "But trust me, there's nothing to worry about. I just need to work out some things in my own mind, okay?"

"Did Vic do something to hurt you?"

Riley hesitated. No, she hadn't. Everyone around her had, but Vic herself made Riley feel wanted. She made her feel loved. Vic hadn't hurt her. Riley was about to say so when they heard someone out in the lobby.

"Hello?" a woman's voice called out. "I'm looking for Riley Warren. Is anyone here?"

Riley sighed in frustration before getting to her feet. Nancy followed her out to the concession stand. Riley's steps faltered when she saw Vera Thayer standing there looking disgusted to even be inside the building.

"There you are," she said when their eyes met. Riley bristled at the self-satisfied grin on Vera's face. "I was worried I'd have to come back later. And trust me, being here once is more than enough."

"What the hell do you want?" Riley asked, happy the snack counter was between them. She had the urge to slug the woman.

"It's come to my attention that you were in New York City visiting Victoria," Vera said, her tone perfectly telegraphing how she felt about it. "I just want to make sure you stay away from her. Someone of Victoria's standing can't be seen with someone…so undesirable."

"Okay, you know what?" Nancy asked as she stormed around the counter to grab Vera by the elbow. "You need to get the hell out of here. Now."

"Let go of me," Vera said as she yanked her arm away. "Do you have any idea who I am?"

"Yes, I do." Nancy was pissed. Riley had never seen her so angry.

"This has nothing to do with you." Vera looked at her as though Nancy was nothing more than a bug to be stepped on. She pushed her out of the way and returned to the counter. "You will leave Victoria alone, do you understand me?"

"I understand you perfectly," Riley said, working hard to keep her voice even. It would be so easy to grab her and slam her head into the counter. She took a deep breath to calm herself. "I also understand that you know absolutely nothing about Vic. If you did, you'd know she doesn't like being called Victoria. She's a grown woman, and she can make her own decisions. If she wants to be with me, then she will be. Do *you* understand *me*?"

"How dare you speak to me that way," Vera said, her face turning red with anger. "Victoria will marry a man and settle down one day. In her heart she knows what's expected of her. If you don't stay away from her, I will make your life miserable. And believe me, I can do it."

"You need to get the *fuck* out of here before I throw you out on your privileged ass." Nancy said the words quietly, but not so quiet Riley didn't hear the word Nancy had never uttered in front of her before.

Vera obviously wasn't used to anyone using the language in front of her because she simply stared at Nancy for a moment before backing away. She looked at Riley again as she reached the door.

"Stay away from her."

Riley fought the urge to run after her and start a physical fight in the parking lot. Nancy turned to her, shaking her head.

"That bitch is a piece of work."

"You need to stop with the swearing, Nancy," Riley said, her tone teasing. "Andy would wash your mouth out with soap if he could hear you right now."

"Please," Nancy said, waving a hand dismissively. "He'd be right there with me on this one, trust me. I can't believe the nerve of that woman."

"I guess it's something I have in common with Vic," Riley said. "We both have mothers who are bitches."

Riley felt her phone vibrate in her pocket and she pulled it out. It was Vic. She almost swiped to answer, but instead ignored the call and shoved it back in her pocket. She let out a breath and turned to go back into the office.

"Whose call did you just ignore?" Nancy said, following her again.

"No one," Riley said. She grabbed her keys off the desk and turned to leave. She shouldn't even have been there anyway. She wasn't scheduled to work until that evening. She'd hoped she might be able to keep her mind off Vic if she went to work all day.

Obviously, that hadn't worked out.

CHAPTER TWENTY-EIGHT

It was a couple of weeks later when the phone ringing in the middle of the night woke Riley from a dead sleep. She grabbed for it and took a moment to see who it was before swiping the screen to answer.

"Riley, you need to come to the hospital," Megan said before she could even say hello.

"What happened?" Riley asked, already up and pulling on a pair of jeans. "Are you okay?"

"It isn't me. It's your mother."

Riley stopped getting dressed and sat on the edge of the bed with a sigh. "She doesn't want me there. I'm not going to show up just so she can tell me to get the hell out."

"Riley, you don't understand," Megan said, sounding almost desperate. "You need to get here. Now."

"Don't you remember last time?"

"Riley, please trust me when I say you have to get here as quickly as you can." Megan said, sounding desperate.

Riley's heart sped up and she almost dropped the phone when she heard the utter despair in Megan's voice. She looked at the clock on her bedside table for the first time and saw she'd only been asleep for an hour. "What happened?"

"It was a car accident."

"I knew she wouldn't really stop drinking." Riley's breath caught in her throat. "Oh, Jesus, was she driving? Did she kill someone?"

"She wasn't driving, Riley. She was in an Uber. They were hit head-on by another vehicle. The driver of the other car was drunk."

Riley had to stifle the laugh that threatened to bubble up. How ironic that her mother, a drunk, was injured in an accident by a drunk driver. To her horror, instead of a laugh, it came out as a sob, and she roughly wiped the tears from her cheek.

"The Uber driver was killed instantly," Megan said. "Your mother was in bad shape when we got there, and she'd lost a lot of blood. Just as we got to the hospital her blood pressure bottomed out and her heart stopped. We got her back, and they rushed her into surgery. Her chances of survival are low, Riley. You have to get here as soon as possible."

"I'm on my way," Riley said before ending the call. She sat there for a moment, and all she could think was how much she wanted to call Vic. She hadn't spoken to her at all since leaving the city, but not because Vic hadn't tried. In fact, she'd been calling every single day and leaving messages, but Riley refused to call her back. It was better this way. The hurt was minimized by walking away before they got too heavily involved.

Yeah, right.

"Are you sure you're all right?" Megan asked the next morning as she drove them back home. Her partner had taken their rig back and left her at the hospital when their shift was over because Riley hadn't felt like driving.

Her mother had passed away at four thirty-eight that morning without ever regaining consciousness after the accident. Riley knew she should mourn—hell, she *wanted* to mourn—but it was almost as though she couldn't be bothered. Every time she felt like she was going to cry because of the loss, she'd remember some of the things her mother had said and done to her over the years and end up feeling nothing but anger.

"Riley?" Megan asked, placing a hand on her knee.

"I'm fine, yeah," she said with a nod and a forced smile. Then the thought hit her that she was going to have to pay for a funeral. And she'd have to make time to clean out the mobile home and try to sell it. There was no way she'd get enough for it to even pay for half of what she was going to have to take care of. The place was in horrible condition. As far as she was concerned, it was uninhabitable. Hell, it was when she was still living there in high school.

"You're staying home from work tonight," Megan said, sounding firm. Riley didn't argue. "I'm off tonight. We'll order a pizza and watch crappy movies, all right?"

"Sure." Riley leaned her head against the seat and closed her eyes. Once they got home, Megan went to the kitchen to cook them some breakfast and Riley sat at the kitchen table, still in a bit of a haze. She knew it was mostly from the lack of sleep rather than because she'd just lost the only family she had. Her mother had never talked about her side of the family, so Riley had never met any aunts, uncles, cousins, or grandparents. She wasn't even sure any of them existed.

"Do you need me to do anything?" Megan asked when she sat down with plates of eggs and bacon in front of them. "I can help with any arrangements that need to be made. I could call the insurance company and credit card companies. Just let me know what you need."

"She didn't have insurance," Riley said with a shake of her head. She looked at Megan and they both started to laugh. "And credit cards? Are you crazy? She couldn't even keep a job for more than a few weeks. The only reason she even had a place to live was because she paid the trailer off before she stopped giving a damn about anything. And I don't even *want* to know how she got money to pay the park for lot rent every month."

Just thinking about it made her head hurt. Megan agreed to call Nancy to let her know Riley wouldn't be in to work that night, and Riley went to her room to take a nap. She didn't think she'd be able to sleep, but when she opened her eyes again it was three in the afternoon. She showered before heading back downstairs and joining Megan on the couch.

"What did Nancy say?" she asked.

"She told me to give you her condolences and not to worry about a thing. She'll make sure everything keeps running at the theater for as long as you need to take off."

"She's been a great friend to me ever since high school, you know?"

"I do know," Megan said. "There are a lot of people in this town who care about you, Riley. You know that, don't you?"

Riley was spared having to respond when the front doorbell rang. She went and opened the door, surprised to see Andy standing there.

"How are you doing?" he asked.

"I'm okay," Riley said with a nod. And she really was. She stepped aside and motioned for him to come in. They went to the living room and sat on the couch. Megan squeezed her shoulder briefly as she excused herself and went to her room.

"Nancy asked me to come over here and discuss something with you," he said. "She would have come herself if she could have gotten someone else to open the theater today."

"What's going on?" Riley asked, wondering what else could go wrong this day. "Is Nancy okay? Are you?"

"We're fine," he said with a wave of his hand. "Back when your mother first started drinking, and it became obvious you were being neglected, Nancy and I put some money away for you in case you needed it someday. It isn't a lot, but it would be enough to pay for a funeral."

"I can't ask you to pay for this," Riley said, shaking her head. "I'll finance the cost if I have to, but this isn't anyone's responsibility but my own."

"Nancy thought you'd say something like that," he said with a chuckle as he pulled a bank book out of his back pocket and held it out to her. "This has all the information you need to see we really did open this account, with your name on it, back in 1996. The interest is minimal, but we did add some money a couple of times over the years. We want you to have it, Riley. You don't have to do this on your own."

She took the book and opened it, seeing her name was indeed on the account, and it was opened when she was fourteen. She stared at the amount, thinking she had to be seeing it wrong. "Ten thousand dollars?" Her throat felt as though it was closing, and her eyes filled with tears. She shook her head. "I can't take this."

"Listen to me," Andy said, taking her hand between his. He waited until Riley met his gaze. "You know Nancy and I never had kids. You were always like a daughter to us, and you still are. You always will be. We want you to take this money to pay for the funeral, and to at least help to pay off any outstanding bills your mother might have had. Please, let us do this for you."

Riley finally nodded after a few moments of thinking how wonderful this man was. She never expected anything from him or Nancy, but this gesture was so like them. She thanked whoever was responsible for putting them in her life. God only knew where she might have ended up if it wasn't for them.

"We know how you felt about your mother, Riley, but no matter your relationship with her, I know her death had to create a vacuum in your life." He put his arms around her and held her as she began to cry. Not for her loss, but for the incredible generosity.

But he was right. There did seem to be a hole in her life now, knowing she would never see her mother again. Never speak to her on the phone again. It was a loss, even though it wasn't. She realized she could now mourn the relationship she always wanted but never had with her mother.

"Thank you for this," she said as she pulled away from him. She wiped the tears from her cheeks and took a deep breath. "I love you guys."

"We love you too, honey," he said with a smile. He placed his hands on his knees. "I should probably get going. Let us know when the service is, because we both want to be there for you."

"I will," she said, even though she was pretty sure she'd just have her cremated. No one other than Andy, Nancy, and Megan would show up for a service anyway. She walked him to the door and hugged him again before he left.

Her phone vibrated in her pocket as she was heading toward Megan's room, so she stopped and pulled it out of her pocket. Vic. Again. Her finger hovered over answer, but she sighed as she swiped ignore. As much as she wanted to hear her voice, she just wasn't ready to talk to her quite yet.

CHAPTER TWENTY-NINE

Vic sighed as she drove to the property she'd purchased in Summerville, a town about twenty minutes northeast of Wolf Bay. The house on the land was big—nearly twenty-five hundred square feet—and she had hopes that Riley might one day agree to live there with her. She waved at the foreman for the crew doing the renovations inside. He was a friend of the family, and her father had arranged for all the work she wanted to be done.

"Vic, it's good to see you again," he said as he shook her hand with a big smile.

"You too, Philip," she said with a nod before looking at the house. "How's it going?"

"Pretty damn good actually. I've had a full crew here seven days a week for the past three weeks. I think we'll be finished ahead of schedule. You want to see what we've done?"

She followed him into the house through the two-car garage. The door opened into the kitchen, which had been fully updated with granite countertops and stainless steel appliances. From the breakfast bar you could see the entire first floor, which consisted of a dining area and a large living room with floor to ceiling windows. And a humongous fireplace she would love sitting in front of during the snowy part of year. Especially if she was lucky enough to have Riley there by her side.

She cautioned herself to not get her hopes up, but she couldn't help dreaming. She hadn't even spoken to Riley in close to a month because she wouldn't answer her calls. In fact, she must have blocked her number, because whenever she called, it went straight to voice mail. She planned on dropping in at the theater once this house was ready to move into and do everything possible to make things right with her.

The upstairs held two bedrooms, with the master suite taking up half the floor. It also featured floor to ceiling windows. There were two huge walk-in closets and a bathroom that was almost as big as the bedroom itself. There was a huge walk-in shower with two showerheads, one of them a rainfall because Riley had fallen in love with the one at her penthouse. The bathroom floor was heated, something Vic insisted on since it could get so damn cold in the winter. There was a Jacuzzi tub and double sinks with a large mirror and a ton of counter space.

Unfortunately, there was no rooftop swimming pool, but the backyard sported an Olympic sized pool and an eight-person hot tub. The entire property was well over three acres, and the closest neighbor was almost a mile away, so privacy wasn't a concern, but she still opted to put in a privacy fence around the spacious backyard.

"I think you're really going to like it here," Philip said as they stood beside the pool. "It's quiet, and there are deer all over the place in the mornings. It's very peaceful."

"I'm happy with the work you've done," she told him, turning to head back into the house. "And you think you'll be completely finished in two weeks?"

"My best guess? We'll be out of here in the next seven to ten days, tops."

She shook his hand again and headed back to her car. She really wanted to see Riley but questioned whether it would be better to wait. She shook her head as she started the engine and decided to just head back to her hotel room. She'd need to go back to the city for the closing on the sale of her penthouse in two days, and then she wouldn't have to return to the city ever again if she didn't want to.

So, she was a little perplexed to find herself pulling into Riley's driveway twenty minutes later. She really had planned on going to the hotel, but her mind seemed to have its own agenda. She didn't even remember turning toward Riley's instead of her hotel. She shut the engine off and walked to the door, knowing that because it was Monday, Riley probably had the day off, but she noticed her car wasn't there.

"Well, fuck me," Megan said when she opened the door and saw Vic standing on the porch. She chuckled then and held up a hand. "And, no, that wasn't an invitation."

"I didn't think it was," Vic said with a slight smile. "Is Riley here?"

"No, she left a few hours ago to drive into the city to see you. Hence the expletive when I found you on the doorstep." Megan stepped aside and motioned for her to enter. "Can I get you something to drink?"

"Water would be great." Vic looked at the time on her phone and sighed. "When exactly did she leave?"

"Not sure. I was asleep when she left. I'm working second shift this week." She shrugged and handed Vic a glass filled with water.

"Can you call her? Maybe she didn't leave that long ago, and she can turn around and come back." Vic hesitated a moment as the words Megan had spoken sunk in. She felt true optimism for the first time in weeks. "Wait, she was going there to see me?"

"She misses you," Megan said with a nod as she presumably looked for Riley's number before putting the phone to her ear. "I've been telling her she needs to sit down and talk to you about everything, but she can be so damned stubborn sometimes. She isn't answering."

"Fuck," Vic muttered. There was no point in her trying if Riley wasn't even picking up for Megan.

"Yeah, I told her she should call you before just going there out of the blue." Megan led her into the living room where they sat on the couch. "Stubborn and impulsive. Not really a good combination. So why are you here?"

"I don't live in the city anymore. I sold my place there and bought a house in Summerville. I'm closing on the penthouse on Wednesday." She was more than a little stunned to learn Riley was going to see her without calling first. "I've been trying to get in touch with her every day, Megan. It goes right to voice mail."

"Do you leave a message?"

"Every freaking time."

"Have you tried telling her you love her?"

"Not something you say for the first time over the phone, especially on a message."

"You're a romantic." Megan smiled, seeming to be pleased at the idea. "That's so sweet."

"You said she misses me?" Vic was skeptical. If she missed her, why would she avoid her calls and texts?

"Oh, my God, I've never seen her so down in the dumps."

"Vanessa told me a little of what happened the night she left the city, but can you tell me what Riley said?"

Megan just stared at her for a moment, no doubt wondering if she'd be betraying any confidences. She must have decided it was okay because she sat back, crossed her legs, and began talking.

Vic was furious by the time she was done, and she stood to pace the living room floor, running her hand through her hair in frustration.

"Seriously? Lisa told her I was bisexual? And that Tyler and I are an item?" Vic blew out a breath and shook her head. "And she overheard Vanessa telling Harper I was only having a bit of fun and would eventually marry a man someday? No wonder she won't answer my calls."

"Hey, don't shoot the messenger. I only know what she told me." Megan held her hands up. "And another tidbit for you—your mother showed up at the theater the morning after Riley drove back, basically telling her the same thing."

"Are you fucking serious right now?" Vic clenched her fists in her lap. She was going to kill Vera someday.

"For what it's worth, she didn't truly believe any of it."

"Then why won't she talk to me?"

"You have to understand the shit her mother put her through," Megan said softly. "She has serious self-esteem issues. She saw those women hanging all over you that night in New York, and she thought she could never measure up. That she'd never have any hope of keeping someone like you happy. So even though she didn't believe what they said, it struck a chord deep inside her."

"I need to go find her," Vic said as she started for the front door.

"Why don't you just wait here?" Megan suggested, following her. "She'll come back home when she finds out you don't live there anymore. I have to leave for work in a few minutes, so sit and make yourself comfortable, all right? Trust me, she'll be happy to see you when she walks in tonight."

Vic hated waiting around, but she nodded. It would be foolish to run after her only to pass her somewhere along the way when she was heading home. Megan handed her the remote for the TV and squeezed her shoulder briefly before going to finish getting ready for work. An idea struck Vic, and she quickly pulled out her phone.

CHAPTER THIRTY

R iley stood in front of Vic's building wondering if she was really doing the right thing. Maybe Vic wouldn't even want to see her. She shook her head and took a deep breath, knowing that wouldn't be the case. Vic tried calling her every day since Riley had left the city without so much as a word to her. After her mother died, she'd programmed her phone to send Vic's calls straight to voice mail without ringing, and Vic had still left messages every single time. And Riley had listened to them, even though she'd swore to herself she wouldn't.

Vic implored her to call her back, to just give her five minutes of her time. But Riley hadn't seen the point. She'd convinced herself she had nothing to give her and Vic was better off without her. But a funny thing happened over the past week or so. She realized she couldn't live without Vic. Despite her best efforts not to, she'd fallen in love with her, and being away from her, not talking to her, caused an actual physical pain in her chest.

Before she could change her mind, she pulled the door open and walked into the lobby. The doorman smiled at her as she approached the desk.

"Can I help you, ma'am?" he asked.

"I'm here to see Victoria Thayer," she said, sounding much more confident than she felt. "Could you please let her know Riley Warren is here?"

"I'm sorry, but Ms. Thayer isn't here." The man shook his head and held out his palms.

"Do you know when she'll be back?" It was three o'clock in the afternoon on a Monday. Of course she'd be at work.

"No, what I mean is she doesn't live here any longer. She sold her penthouse and moved out."

"What?" Riley felt the words like a punch in the gut. Vic had never said anything to her about moving in any of the messages she'd left. But really, why would she have with Riley acting like a child and refusing to talk to her. How stupid of her to drive all this way without calling her first. "Do you have any idea where she went?"

"I'm sorry, but no," he said, seeming to be truly regretful that he couldn't help her. "She left no forwarding address."

"How long ago did she leave?"

"Two weeks, I think?"

Riley just stared at him for a moment in disbelief, realizing Vic had probably been gone when Riley's mother died. She wasn't sure how long she would have stood there if the doors behind her hadn't opened.

"Oh, thank God," said someone as they entered. Riley turned to look and saw it was Vanessa. "I was worried I'd be too late to catch you."

"How would you even know I was here?" Riley asked, truly perplexed.

"If you'd ever answer your phone, you'd know," she said with a huff. "Come have a cup of coffee with me. We need to talk."

Riley hesitated, not sure she wanted to go anywhere with her. She shook her head and looked at the time. "I really should get back home."

"Seriously?" Vanessa laughed as she stepped into her personal space and took her by the arm as she led her to the door. "You're telling me you drove all this way just to, what? Tell Vic you had to turn around and get back home?"

Riley didn't even bother to answer, knowing anything she might say would probably sound equally as ridiculous. She allowed Vanessa to lead her down the sidewalk and into a small coffee shop a few doors down. Neither of them said anything until they had cups in hand and found a vacant table in a back corner.

"So, Megan tried to call you and you didn't answer. She wanted to tell you that Vic is at your house. And Vic, of course, didn't even bother calling because she said you never answer anymore when she does." Vanessa took a tentative sip of her coffee and sighed. "So, Vic phoned me to come and try to find you."

"Why is she at my house?" Riley asked, stunned. "And where did she move to?"

"Again, if you'd answer your phone, you'd know these things." She tapped her manicured nails on the table as she seemed to think on it for a moment. "Okay, let's start over. I need to apologize to you. For so many things. First, for treating you the way I did in high school. You never did anything to me, or to anyone I knew, to deserve it. We were bored and wanted someone to pick on. You were there. I'm not trying to excuse any of it but am simply stating a fact. I fully intended to say that to you at the reunion, but you and Vic ran off, and I barely saw you again after that."

"I appreciate the apology," Riley said, looking down at her hands which she had wrapped around her warm cup. "I'm not sure I can ever forgive some of the shit that happened, especially the taunts that I should just kill myself. I almost did, you know."

"Fuck," Vanessa said, shaking her head. Riley met her gaze and was surprised to see she was on the verge of tears. Vanessa dabbed at her eyes with a napkin. "I really am *so* sorry."

"Thank you." Riley felt tears of her own threatening, but she somehow managed to keep them from falling.

"And thank you. For saving my life. It scares the hell out of me to think I could have actually died that night. And you rushed right in there without any thought to your own safety and pulled me out." Vanessa glanced down at Riley's arm and reached out to touch the scars before her eyes welled up again. She grabbed another napkin. "Shit. I haven't cried this much in I don't know how long. Even at my wedding. So anyway, I'm sorry you got hurt saving me."

"It wasn't your fault." Riley shook her head and touched the hand that was still on her arm. "I saw the accident happen. I knew when I saw the fire in your car that you'd never make it if you had to wait for the paramedics."

"Did you know it was me?" Vanessa asked, chuckling. "I'm sure if you had you wouldn't have risked your own life."

"I didn't know until I got you away from the car, and even then, I wasn't one hundred percent sure if it was you or Vic. But nothing else mattered in the moment besides getting you out of danger."

"I feel like the next one might be the biggest apology," Vanessa said, sitting back in her chair. "I didn't know you were in the bathroom that night at the movie theater."

"How…" Riley began, but stopped because she wasn't even sure what to say.

"Megan told Vic, and Vic was furious at me when she called to ask me to find you."

"Would it have made a difference if you'd known I'd overheard you?"

"Yes, even if you don't want to believe it." Vanessa leaned forward and stared at her coffee cup. "There are still a lot of people in the world who are ignorant and hateful when it comes to gays and lesbians. When I'm in Wolf Bay, I feel like I need to make those people believe Vic isn't really gay. I hate that I feel that way, but I think a lot of it comes from my mother being so disdainful of her. I feel like everyone in that damn town is the same way. I'm so sorry you overheard what I was saying, and I hope someday you can find it in your heart to forgive me."

Riley stared at her for a moment before finally looking away. Vanessa reached across the table and touched her arm again, and Riley looked at her, trying to tamp down her anger. This woman couldn't know the feelings her words had brought to the surface for Riley, and even though she was dealing with them, it still hurt.

"What about the night in New York City?"

"I can't take the blame for any of that. The things that were said to you were way out of line, and I had no idea what Tara and Lisa said until the next day. I think Tara's always been attracted to Vic, and she let her jealousy show."

"I overheard Vic telling Lisa I was leaving the next morning, and they should have dinner or drinks, or something, after I was gone." Riley held Vanessa's gaze to see if she was going to make up some excuse, but she just smiled, which irked Riley. "Are you going to try and tell me it was all innocent?"

"It was," Vanessa said with a nod. "Lisa is our cousin. Her part of the family has always resented us because our father inherited the business instead of his brother. We try to keep the lines of communications open through her."

"Well, it certainly seemed as though you set it all up," Riley said.

"I know, and believe me, I heard it all from Vic that night because she thought the exact same thing. Honestly? We haven't spoken a whole lot since." Vanessa sighed and then offered a rueful smile. "I just hope she and I can get past this somehow. And you, too. I swear to God, if you two talk things out and end up back together, I will be your biggest champion, especially when it comes to my mother."

"I should go," Riley said, seeing by the clock on the wall it was approaching four o'clock. Not that traffic was ever any good in the city, but if she waited much longer, she'd end up in the worst of it. "Thank you for this. I appreciate you taking the time to clear the air."

"For what it's worth, I hope you do end up with Vic." Vanessa stood and pulled her into an embrace, much to Riley's surprise. It took her a moment to relax into it, but she finally hugged her back. "I've never seen her as happy as she was with you." She stepped back and laughed softly. "And I've never seen her as miserable as she was this past month without you."

"Thank you," Riley said again, mostly because she didn't know what else to say, and if she had to deal with much more of Vanessa being sappy with her, she'd probably start crying. She rushed outside and headed for her car, intent on driving straight home without making any stops. She pulled her phone out as she walked and dialed Vic's number. She answered on the first ring.

"Riley?" she said, sounding frantic.

"Jesus, Vic, are you sitting on your phone?" Riley asked with a chuckle. She unlocked her car door and slid in before closing her eyes and letting the sound of Vic's voice wash over her. God, she'd missed her.

"Pretty much, yeah," she answered. "Did Vanessa find you?"

"She did, and I'm leaving the city as soon as I can fight through the traffic. Will you still be around when I get home? We need to talk."

"Megan told me to wait here for you, so I'm watching your TV and eating your junk food."

"I wish I were there with you," Riley said with a smile.

"You will be soon enough. Drive carefully, all right? Those people in the city are shitty drivers."

"I'll keep it in mind." Riley started the car and they said their good-byes before she dropped the phone on the seat next to her and headed out of the garage she'd parked in. She knew she was smiling like an idiot, and she didn't even care.

CHAPTER THIRTY-ONE

Vic began pacing when the clock said it was eight fifteen and Riley wasn't there yet. She went to look out the window at the driveway, but hers was still the only car there. She paced a few minutes more before she heard a car door slam. She knew she should be sitting on the couch and acting as though seeing Riley again wasn't affecting her, but she couldn't help it. She stood just inside the front door and waited.

Riley jumped back when the door opened and she was face-to-face with Vic, and she placed a hand over her own heart.

"Jesus Christ, you scared the hell out of me," she said. Vic grabbed her by the hand and pulled her inside before pushing the door closed. Riley smiled at her. "Hello."

"I've missed you so much, Riley," Vic said as she held her close and nuzzled her neck. "I hope you weren't coming here to tell me you never want to see me again, because that would be a little awkward now."

"Technically, I was coming here because I live here," Riley said, hugging her back just as tightly. "But there is something I want to tell you."

"Uh-oh," Vic said, stepping back a couple feet. "Maybe we should sit down for this."

Riley didn't argue, which worried Vic a bit. She hadn't realized how off kilter her world was until she held Riley in her arms just now. Everything felt centered again, but now the dread of what Riley might say was threatening to tip everything again. They sat next to each other on the couch, and Riley held her hand as she faced her and met her eyes.

"First of all, did Megan tell you my mother died?" Riley asked.

"Oh, my God, Riley, I'm so sorry," Vic said, fighting the need to pull her into an embrace. "Megan didn't say anything, but she did tell me what my mother said to you."

"I handled Vera," Riley said with a small grin. "Well, Nancy did, anyway. You should have seen it. She was swearing like a sailor."

"I'm sure Vera was appalled," Vic said with a chuckle. "I'm glad you didn't let her get the better of you. I'll deal with her and make sure she knows not to bother you again. So, how did your mother die?"

"Believe it or not, she was killed by a drunk driver." Riley laughed, because how could she not? The irony of it all was too much. They sat in silence for a couple of minutes, just holding hands and looking at each other. Riley took a deep breath before speaking again. "Why didn't you tell me you were moving out of the city in any of those messages you left?"

"Would it have mattered?" Vic asked with a shrug. "Why didn't you answer any of my calls?"

"Point taken. But, yes, it might have mattered. I certainly wouldn't have wasted an entire day driving there and back to find you. Where did you move to?"

"Vanessa didn't tell you?"

"We got sidetracked with apologies and she never did even though I asked. I was so ready to head back here I forgot to ask again before I left."

"When I was here for the three weeks leading up to her wedding, I was in touch with a Realtor to see what the market had to offer in the area." Vic looked at their clasped hands as she spoke, not trusting quite yet that Riley would react favorably to what she was about to say. "They showed me a house in Summerville, and I fell in love with it. I closed on the sale about five weeks ago, and there are contractors there doing some renovations as we speak. I'll be moving into it in a couple of weeks."

"Wait, what?" Riley was obviously surprised, but Vic couldn't tell if it was a happy surprise or not. "Summerville? Like twenty minutes from here? *That* Summerville?"

"Yes. I moved out of the penthouse a couple of weeks ago and have been living in a hotel ever since. I quit my job, Riley."

"Not because of me?"

"No, but I'll admit knowing you were here made it an easier decision. I first contacted the Realtor before I ever saw you again, and I'd been thinking about quitting for quite some time. I just needed the right motivation to finally do it."

"Not many people could be unemployed and buy a new house at the same time." Riley sounded skeptical, and Vic finally looked at her. She was happy to see a smile on her face.

"Are you okay with me not having a steady income?" Vic asked and held her breath waiting for the answer.

"I told you I don't care about your money," Riley said, smoothing her fingers along Vic's jawline. "I've lived my entire life not having more than a few hundred dollars in the bank at any given time, and I can do it for the rest of my life if I have to."

"I love you, Riley," she said, staring into her eyes. Her heart had never felt so full. "I think I fell in love with you back in high school."

Riley straddled her and framed her face between her hands as she kissed her. Vic was instantly aroused when their tongues met in a duel for control. Her hands went to Riley's ass and squeezed, causing Riley to surge against her which effectively broke the kiss.

"I love you, too," Riley said with a smile. They were both breathing heavily, and it was all Vic could do to not rip her clothes off and have her way with her right then and there. Riley ran a thumb along Vic's lower lip. "I fell in love with you the first time you tried to stand up for me against your sister and her friends. I just wish I'd had the courage to tell you then."

"I'm just glad you have the opportunity to tell me now."

"Come upstairs with me?" Riley asked. "I don't want to let you go just yet."

❖

"Hey, baby?" Vic said quietly, not wanting to wake her up if she was sleeping. It was after three in the morning according to the clock on the bedside table, and they'd only fallen asleep about thirty minutes earlier. "You awake?"

"Hmmm," Riley murmured as she pressed her ass into Vic's hips, causing Vic to catch her breath. "What time is it?"

"It's after three," she answered as she tightened her hold around Riley's torso.

"Just can't get enough of me, huh?"

"Never," she said, not surprised in the least to realize it was true. "But that isn't why I asked if you were awake."

Riley turned in her arms so she was on her back and Vic was looking down at her. Vic ran the backs of her fingers across her cheek and gazed into her eyes. She fought the desire to take her again, because there was something she needed to tell her, and she wasn't sure how she was going to react.

"Is everything okay?" Riley asked, looking concerned.

"Perfect." Vic smiled at her before placing a quick kiss on her lips. She decided to just say it and get it out there. "I talked to Steve, the guy who owns the movie theater you work at. I inquired about purchasing it."

"You did what?" Riley sat up and leaned against the headboard but didn't bother to cover her breasts when the sheet fell away. "Why the hell would you do that?"

"I know how much you want it, and I want to give it to you, if you'll let me." Vic sat up and folded her legs underneath her so she could face Riley.

"No," Riley said, shaking her head. "I can't believe you'd go behind my back like this. I told you I don't want your money."

"Just listen to me for a second, all right?" Vic waited and watched as Riley looked like she was going to blow a gasket, but she finally nodded and folded her arms over her chest. "If it makes you more comfortable, I can loan you the money. You can make payments to me if you want to, although it seems kind of silly."

"Silly?" Riley blurted out. "Why the hell would it be silly?"

"Because I want you to move in with me," Vic said softly. She watched in amazement as all the fight went out of Riley's expression. "I love you, and I can't imagine living my life without you being there every day. I want to build a life with you, Riley. I want us to grow old together."

"You aren't proposing, are you?"

"Someday I probably will, but no, not right now." The thought had crossed her mind, but she knew it was way too soon. Maybe in a couple of years she'd revisit the idea. "And the reason I want to buy it for you is *because* you don't want my money. It doesn't matter if I ever work another day in my life. I have more money than we could ever need or want. But what I want most is to make you unbelievably happy."

"Megan told you she's moving to California, didn't she?" Riley was crying and trying to wipe the tears away that were falling faster than she could deal with.

"What? No, she didn't say a word," Vic said, moving to sit next to her and pulling her closer so Riley had her head on her shoulder. "I swear she didn't."

"I wasn't going to be able to afford this place on my own. I thought I was going to be homeless. Or be forced to move back into that damned trailer, and that would have been a horrendous situation all the way around." Riley laughed through her tears, and then she had the hiccups. "You really want me to move in? Are you ready to live with me twenty-four/seven?"

"I just spent the last month without you twenty-four/seven, and I thought it was going to kill me." She pressed a kiss to Riley's head and closed her eyes. "I really, really want you to move in with me. If you think you can stand me being around all the time."

"I don't suppose it has a rooftop pool?" Riley twisted to look at her with a wry grin.

"No, but there is a huge pool in the very private and secluded backyard. And did I mention the hot tub? Heated floors in the bathrooms *and* the kitchen. Your own walk-in closet is almost the size of this room. And floor to ceiling windows with views to rival that of the cityscape." Vic looked into her eyes and smiled. "I love you, Riley Warren. More than I could ever put into words. Will you move in with me?"

"How can I pass up everything you just described?" Riley asked as she straddled Vic's hips and leaned over so her breasts were close to Vic's face. "The fact you'll be there too? Just icing on the cake. I love you, Victoria Thayer."

She covered Vic's mouth with her own then, and Vic did all she could to convey exactly how she felt in that kiss. But how could she, really? The reality of being with Riley far exceeded all of the hopes and dreams she'd ever had.

About the Author

PJ Trebelhorn was born and raised in the greater metropolitan area of Portland, Oregon. Her love of sports (mainly baseball and ice hockey) was fueled in part by her father's interests. She likes to brag about the fact that her uncle managed the Milwaukee Brewers for five years, and the Chicago Cubs for one year.

PJ now resides in western New York with her wife, Cheryl; their three cats; and one very neurotic dog. When not writing or reading, PJ enjoys watching movies and spending too much time playing on the Playstation. She's still a huge fan of the Flyers, Phillies, and Eagles, even though she's now in Sabres and Bills territory.

PJ can be contacted at PJTrebelhorn@gmail.com.

Books Available from Bold Strokes Books

A Love that Leads to Home by Ronica Black. For Carla Sims and Janice Carpenter, home isn't about location, it's where your heart is. (978-1-63555-675-9)

Blades of Bluegrass by D. Jackson Leigh. A US Army occupational therapist must rehab a bitter veteran who is a ticking political time bomb the military is desperate to disarm. (978-1-63555-637-7)

Guarding Hearts by Jaycie Morrison. As treachery and temptation threaten the women of the Women's Army Corps, who will risk it all for love? (978-1-63555-806-7)

Hopeless Romantic by Georgia Beers. Can a jaded wedding planner and an optimistic divorce attorney possibly find a future together? (978-1-63555-650-6)

Hopes and Dreams by PJ Trebelhorn. Movie theater manager Riley Warren is forced to face her high school crush and tormentor, wealthy socialite Victoria Thayer, at their twentieth reunion. (978-1-63555-670-4)

In the Cards by Kimberly Cooper Griffin. Daria and Phaedra are about to discover that love finds a way, especially when powers outside their control are at play. (978-1-63555-717-6)

Moon Fever by Ileandra Young. SPEAR agent Danika Karson must clear her werewolf friend of multiple false charges while teaching her vampire girlfriend to resist the blood mania brought on by a full moon. (978-1-63555-603-2)

Quake City by St John Karp. Can Andre find his best friend Amy before the night devolves into a nightmare of broken hearts, malevolent drag queens, and spontaneous human combustion? Or has it always happened this way, every night, at Aunty Bob's Quake City Club? (978-1-63555-723-7)

Serenity by Jesse J. Thoma. For Kit Marsden, there are many things in life she cannot change. Serenity is in the acceptance. (978-1-63555-713-8)

Sylver and Gold by Michelle Larkin. Working feverishly to find a killer before he strikes again, Boston Homicide Detective Reid Sylver and rookie cop London Gold are blindsided by their chemistry and developing attraction. (978-1-63555-611-7)

Trade Secrets by Kathleen Knowles. In Silicon Valley, love and business are a volatile mix for clinical lab scientist Tony Leung and venture capitalist Sheila Garrison. (978-1-63555-642-1)

Death Overdue by David S. Pederson. Did Heath turn to murder in an alcohol induced haze to solve the problem of his blackmailer, or was it someone else who brought about a death overdue? (978-1-63555-711-4)

Entangled by Melissa Brayden. Becca Crawford is the perfect person to head up the Jade Hotel, if only the captivating owner of the local vineyard would get on board with her plan and stop badmouthing the hotel to everyone in town. (978-1-63555-709-1)

First Do No Harm by Emily Smith. Pierce and Cassidy are about to discover that when it comes to love, sometimes you have to risk it all to have it all. (978-1-63555-699-5)

Kiss Me Every Day by Dena Blake. For Wynn Evans, wishing for a do-over with Carly Jamison was a long shot, actually getting one was a game changer. (978-1-63555-551-6)

Olivia by Genevieve McCluer. In this lesbian Shakespeare adaption with vampires, Olivia is a centuries old vampire who must fight a strange figure from her past if she wants a chance at happiness. (978-1-63555-701-5)

One Woman's Treasure by Jean Copeland. Daphne's search for discarded antiques and treasures leads to an embarrassing misunderstanding, and ultimately, the opportunity for the romance of a lifetime with Nina. (978-1-63555-652-0)

Silver Ravens by Jane Fletcher. Lori has lost her girlfriend, her home, and her job. Things don't improve when she's kidnapped and taken to fairyland. (978-1-63555-631-5)

Still Not Over You by Jenny Frame, Carsen Taite, Ali Vali. Old flames die hard in these tales of a second chance at love with the ex you're still not over. Stories by award winning authors Jenny Frame, Carsen Taite, and Ali Vali. (978-1-63555-516-5)

Storm Lines by Jessica L. Webb. Devon is a psychologist who likes rules. Marley is a cop who doesn't. They don't always agree, but both fight to protect a girl immersed in a street drug ring. (978-1-63555-626-1)

The Politics of Love by Jen Jensen. Is it possible to love across the political divide in a hostile world? Conservative Shelley Whitmore and liberal Rand Thomas are about to find out. (978-1-63555-693-3)

All the Paths to You by Morgan Lee Miller. High school sweethearts Quinn Hughes and Kennedy Reed reconnect five years after they break up and realize that their chemistry is all but over. (978-1-63555-662-9)

Arrested Pleasures by Nanisi Barrett D'Arnuck. When charged with a crime she didn't commit Katherine Lowe faces the question: Which is harder, going to prison or falling in love? (978-1-63555-684-1)

Bonded Love by Renee Roman. Carpenter Blaze Carter suffers an injury that shatters her dreams, and ER nurse Trinity Greene hopes to show her that sometimes love is worth fighting for. (978-1-63555-530-1)

Convergence by Jane C. Esther. With life as they know it on the line, can Aerin McLeary and Olivia Ando's love survive an otherworldly threat to humankind? (978-1-63555-488-5)

Coyote Blues by Karen F. Williams. Riley Dawson, psychotherapist and shape-shifter, has her world turned upside down when Fiona Bell, her one true love, returns. (978-1-63555-558-5)

Drawn by Carsen Taite. Will the clues lead Detective Claire Hanlon to the killer terrorizing Dallas, or will she merely lose her heart to person of interest, urban artist Riley Flynn? (978-1-63555-644-5)

Every Summer Day by Lee Patton. Meant to celebrate every summer day, Luke's journal instead chronicles a love affair as fast-moving and possibly as fatal as his brother's brain tumor. (978-1-63555-706-0)

Lucky by Kris Bryant. Was Serena Evans's luck really about winning the lottery, or is she about to get even luckier in love? (978-1-63555-510-3)

The Last Days of Autumn by Donna K. Ford. Autumn and Caroline question the fairness of life, the cruelty of loss, and what it means to love as they navigate the complicated minefield of relationships, grief, and life-altering illness. (978-1-63555-672-8)

Three Alarm Response by Erin Dutton. In the midst of tragedy, can these first responders find love and healing? Three stories of courage, bravery, and passion. (978-1-63555-592-9)

Veterinary Partner by Nancy Wheelton. Callie and Lauren are determined to keep their hearts safe but find that taking a chance on love is the safest option of all. (978-1-63555-666-7)

Everyday People by Louis Barr. When film star Diana Danning hires private eye Clint Steele to find her son, Clint turns to his former West Point barracks mate, and ex-buddy with benefits, Mars Hauser to lend his cyber espionage and digital black ops skills to the case. (978-1-63555-698-8)

Forging a Desire Line by Mary P. Burns. When Charley's ex-wife, Tricia, is diagnosed with inoperable cancer, the private duty nurse Tricia hires turns out to be the handsome and aloof Joanna, who ignites something inside Charley she isn't ready to face. (978-1-63555-665-0)

Love on the Night Shift by Radclyffe. Between ruling the night shift in the ER at the Rivers and raising her teenage daughter, Blaise Richilieu has all the drama she needs in her life, until a dashing young attending appears on the scene and relentlessly pursues her. (978-1-63555-668-1)

Olivia's Awakening by Ronica Black. When the daring and dangerously gorgeous Eve Monroe is hired to get Olivia Savage into shape, a fierce passion ignites, causing both to question everything they've ever known about love. (978-1-63555-613-1)

The Duchess and the Dreamer by Jenny Frame. Clementine Fitzroy has lost her faith and love of life. Can dreamer Evan Fox make her believe in life and dream again? (978-1-63555-601-8)

The Road Home by Erin Zak. Hollywood actress Gwendolyn Carter is about to discover that losing someone you love sometimes means gaining someone to fall for. (978-1-63555-633-9)

Waiting for You by Elle Spencer. When passionate past-life lovers meet again in the present day, one remembers it vividly and the other isn't so sure. (978-1-63555-635-3)

While My Heart Beats by Erin McKenzie. Can a love born amidst the horrors of the Great War survive? (978-1-63555-589-9)

Face the Music by Ali Vali. Sweet music is the last thing that happens when Nashville music producer Mason Liner, and daughter of country royalty Victoria Roddy are thrown together in an effort to save country star Sophie Roddy's career. (978-1-63555-532-5)

Flavor of the Month by Georgia Beers. What happens when baker Charlie and chef Emma realize their differing paths have led them right back to each other? (978-1-63555-616-2)

Mending Fences by Angie Williams. Rancher Bobbie Del Rey and veterinarian Grace Hammond are about to discover if heartbreaks of the past can ever truly be mended. (978-1-63555-708-4)

Silk and Leather: Lesbian Erotica with an Edge edited by Victoria Villasenor. This collection of stories by award winning authors offers fantasies as soft as silk and tough as leather. The only question is: How far will you go to make your deepest desires come true? (978-1-63555-587-5)